"A glooming peace this sorrow will not show its head. (sad things: some shall be pardoned, and some punished: for never was a story of more woe than this of Juliet and her Romeo."

Star Tossed

Michael closed the dusty tome and leaned back on his elbows. He watched Isabel with furrowed brow as she wiped at her eyes with the back of her hand and sniffled softly. "That was," She said as she looked up through the dappled light filtering through the trees. "I get it now. I get how two people so filled with love for the other could risk everything, even life, for the briefest of time together."

Michael smiled and kissed her softly on the shoulder. "There is something to be said for the Loram and their way of going about living isn't there?" He said as he trailed hot kisses across her shoulder and neck. Isabel leaned back against him and murmured softly. "Mmmm hmm."

Michael reached into the pocket of his hoody and pulled out a small red box, fidgeting with it nervously for a moment. "Isabel," He said quietly and she turned to face him. Just as her lips were to meet his, he held up the box between them.

"Michael?" she whispered, eyes lowered, the box filling her vision.

"The rules be damned Isabel, I've loved you for centuries now. I want you, only you." That said, he opened the box and Isabel gasped.

Nestled in a swaddling of blood red satin, lay a tri gold band with three diamonds. Her hand trembled as she reached for it, eyes darting from the ring to him and back again. She traced the diamonds with her finger and lifted it out of the box. The sunlight glinted off of the words he'd had inscribed on the inside of the band. *'Il mio amore per sempre. Michael'*

"My love forever. Michael." Isabel whispered as the tears she'd been holding off fell unbidden onto her sun kissed cheeks.

Taking the ring from her, Michael placed it on the ring finger of her left hand. "Marry me Isabel, marry me and make me the happiest man on earth."

Isabel stared at it, thoughts tumbling over one another as her mind reeled with reasons to say no, struggling to do so, because her heart was, for the first time in her long existence, having a say of its own. *'Yes,'* Her heart whispered once. *'Yes; say yes, say yes!'* A quiet chant that quickly became her hearts mantra.

"Yes." She breathed as he kissed her. "Yes," The rules be damned. No one…*no one* was going to dictate who she was allowed to love. It may have taken just over three hundred years for him to propose but she was his and that was the end of it.

Isabel stood in front of the restroom mirror, under the wash of the cold florescent lighting and stared at her own reflection. Eyes swollen and red from crying, makeup smudged and running, she had seen better days. The Andromedan council had laid down its decision and as the gavel came crashing down, so had all of her hopes, dreams and desires. There was no appeal, no reprieve or second chances; their verdict was irrevocable and final.

She glanced over her shoulder at her bags which had been packed for her. Gone she knew, was anything that would remind her of him even remotely. Isabel fought back another wave of tears and shouldered her carry on bag. Dragging her suitcase behind her, its wheels clacking over the tiles as she exited the restroom, she made her way over to where her escorts awaited her.

She knew in her heart that the next twenty-four hours would bring her nothing but regret and sadness, beyond those one thousand four hundred and forty minutes lay oblivion.

A life reset.

A life without meaning.

A life without him.

She considered running but a quick glance up and down the concourse derailed that idea. Sentries manned every exit, two to a door and armed to the teeth. Resigned to her fate, she walked slowly to the three women and one man who were to deliver her to the center. Her curse, she thought was not even being allowed the opportunity of the sweet escape that death would afford. She was a true immortal, one who would soon forget everything she'd ever come to know. One who would soon loose all memory of the only man she had ever loved.

Michael walked along the wooded path that ran along the back of his house, down towards the river. This had been one of their favorite spots, shielded by the trees they were allowed to be themselves, far from the prying eyes of the Arcturian prefects or the Andromedan council. He leaned against the tree under which they once sat not that many weeks ago dreaming of a life together.

Balling up his fist he slammed it into the rough bark of the tree, splintering it. He felt his hand shatter and found comfort in the pain. Flexing his fingers, his hand repaired itself almost instantly. *'That was for the Andromedan council.'* He thought and pulled his arm back. He struck again, the tree shuddered and groaned at the impact. "That was for the Arcturian prefects." He spat through clenched teeth and preparing to strike again, sudden anguish stopped him.

Michael leaned into the tree and pressed his forehead against the rough bark allowing the tears to fall. Isabel was everything to him, his breath and his soul and in twenty-four hours she would be lost to him forever. His was a crueler fate, an immortals life full of memories and remembrances. An eternity of aching for the one thing he could never have...her.

2

Patience is a virtue.

That being said, Patience wasn't virtuous by any means. In fact she was the wildest and most manipulative and conniving woman Michael had ever met. There was something about her though, a kindness that surpassed the kindness the Loram were known for.

The Loram were what was left of the human race, a proud people who served immortals in either realm.   Viewed as flawed by both because of their short life spans and their capacity to be ruled by their emotions as well as their logic, the Loram became the go-betweens for the Andromedan council and the Arcturian prefects. Two ruling bodies from two different houses who held nothing but disdain for the other.

Michael and Patience had met on a bright and glorious day when Michael was walking through Tarkon Park, a gathering place for the Loram. Head down, he brooded. Every pore radiating a sinister and deadly vibe, a proverbial dark cloud hanging over his head.

He had just left the priory meeting in Dulam where he and Isabel had been called to account for their crimes against the council and the prefect. *'Crimes...'* Michael thought as he skirted a fountain. *'...Since when was love a crime?'* He'd often wondered what would really happen if the Andromedan council who was governed and ruled by the mind and the Arcturian prefect who was governed and ruled by the heart threw away their differences and embraced each other.

As a child he'd been told that neither could co-exist in harmony nor love without forfeiting their immortality. Michael accepted the reasoning at first but as he grew he rebelled against it, demanding that someone explain to him how two people loving each other could ever be a bad thing regardless of the consequences.

Patience watched him as he strolled past families enjoying a midafternoon picnic, kids playing catch and old people sitting on park benches holding hands. She noticed that the sounds and sights of people laughing, enjoying themselves, made him look all the more miserable. If that were possible. That wouldn't do.

If there was one thing that made her heart ache, one thing that made her angry, it was a hurting soul. House and race and station be damned. This one wasn't going to get away. Not before she'd made him smile at least once.

She approached him and as soon as he saw her, he changed direction only to have her alter her course as well. Finally, after a slow and awkward dance, he stopped and held up his hands in surrender.

"What...?" He said through clenched teeth.

The tall blonde extended her hand and said, "I'm Patience."

Michael glared at her and snorted, "You're fucking kidding me right?"

Patience stood her ground, arm outstretched, hand extended in greeting and smiled wickedly. "Nope, not kidding and you are?"

"Annoyed and wanting to be left alone." Michael said and moved to step around her. Patience matched his move and stuck out her lower lip, pouting. "Christ," Michael said as he ran a hand through his shoulder length brown hair. Sighing he shook her hand and said, "I'm Michael pleased to meet you. Can I go now?"

Patience laughed and the sound almost brought a faint smile to his lips. "Now that wasn't so hard was it?" She asked as she slipped next to him, looping her arm around his. "Coffee...?" She asked as she pulled him along towards the street.

"I'm not sure what the hell you're doing," Michael said as he pulled his arm from her grip. "But no, we are not having coffee. I want to be left alone."

"Sure we are and no you don't." Patience laughed, taking his arm again, her grip more unforgiving. "Why so glum chum?" She asked with a wink.

"You are impossible." Michael ground out. "Fucking Loram and their vast melting pot of logic and emotions. Why couldn't you pick on someone else?"

"If you hadn't noticed, everyone else is in a good mood. You're the only one walking around looking as pissy as a half drowned cat." Patience whispered conspiratorially.

"I'm not getting out of having coffee with you am I?" Michael asked, realizing that he didn't want to be alone after all.

Patience shook her head. "Nope..."

"Fuck. Yeah I figured as much." Michael said. "Fine, one coffee and then you're gone."

"Absolutely!" Patience laughed. "Anything you say, your wish is my command."

Michael quickly resigned himself to Patience' attentive and extroverted manner and before he knew it they were leaning across the table from each other as she listened to his random musings. Patience was living up to her name, had their roles been reversed he would have been tempted to strangle her. But before he knew it, it was a quarter to six and his stomach was rumbling. "I should be going," He said as he drained his fifth café au lait. "I've wasted enough of your time."

Patience arched a perfectly sculptured eyebrow at him and smiled. "From the sounds of it," She said as she glanced down at his stomach, "You're hungry and so am I. I say lets get some supper and after if you still feel like bolting we'll part ways. No harm no foul."

Michael was at once amused and offended. This woman had brass balls and they suited her as did her bright blue eyes and pouting mouth. "Bolting...?" He said gruffly. "Who said I was bolting? I was just thinking that while this has been fun, I've done nothing but complain. You must be bored stiff so I thought the polite thing to do was to put *you* out of *my* misery."

Patience stood and by Christ the woman had the longest legs. No wonder the Loram were bred for sex. Not that he liked long legs on a woman, no, he preferred his women shorter, "fun-sized" as Isabel liked to say. "Come on," Patience said extending her hand to him once again, breaking him out of his reverie. "I'm not done with you yet and I know the best little Italian place across the square."

3

Isabel unpacked her meager belongings slowly, inspecting each item carefully for even the tiniest reminder of Michael. He had promised her that he would get something to her somehow. Something that would jog her memory after the procedure. Tentatively, she removed the last item from the suitcase and stared at it as tears filled her eyes.

The hairbrush held no secrets, certainly nothing of Michael. It was store bought, still in the wrapper and she could kill her mother for it. With a cry she threw it across the room and folded in on herself, slumping to the floor by the bed sobbing. It was really over. Soon Michael wouldn't even be a distant and intangible memory. Soon he, along with every thought, feeling and emotion associated with him would be gone as if they never existed. In all of the centuries she'd known him, he'd never failed her and now when she needed him to succeed most, there was nothing left of him to remind her. Nothing left to start over with.

"Life is always in the tiniest of details Izzy." He'd once told her. "Even the most incredibly obscure thing can jog a persons memory and bring everything back from the edge of oblivion." The deep resonant rumble of his accented voice wasn't something she'd ever forget. The way the sound made her break out in goose bumps and got her heart racing couldn't be done away with now, could it? Still she willed herself to hang on to it.

Finally, Isabel crawled up onto the bed and wept into her pillow until fatigue pulled her down into a fitful sleep.

"You're full of shit!" Patience said in a hushed whisper. "They can't do that can they? And if they can…why the hell haven't I heard of it?"

Michael tore off a piece of garlic bread from the loaf between them and nodded sadly. "They can and they will. Our relationship; our *forbidden* relationship sealed our fate. And the Loram that help with each procedure are carefully screened. Loose lips sink ships and all that stuff."

"Hang on, *Loram* help out with the procedures?"

"Keeps the Andromedan council and the Arcturian prefects hands clean so to speak."

Patience chewed slowly as she ran scenarios through her mind and finally said, "So something as simple as a scrap of paper with 'don't forget me' written on it would work?"

Jesus but the woman changed tracks fast. Michael shook his head and took a sip of his wine. "Not quite that simple, it'd take something like this." He said as he slipped the ring from his finger.

"You were married?" Patience asked, mortified at the thought of two people torn from each others arms only to never be allowed to meet again.

"In our hearts, I was certainly hoping that we could find a Loram to marry us but almost as soon as she'd said yes, the Andromedan council had us in chains."

Patience took the ring. It was a tri gold band with a solitaire diamond embedded in the center. Turning it over, she read the inscription on the inside of the band. Her hand fluttered to her mouth and her eyes filled with tears as she re-read it. "Oh Michael," She said softly. "She did...I know she did."

Michael allowed himself the smallest of smiles and sat back in his seat. He knew the inscription well for as deeply engraved as it was in the precious metal, it was even more so engraved in his heart. It read; *'Michael, always and forever. Isabel'*

4

Isabel awoke with a start, sheets tangled about her lithe five foot three inch frame. She'd been dreaming again, dreaming of the last moments she'd spent with Michael. They'd been nestled in bed just holding each other when the door to the hotel room had exploded inward. Six men burst in, weapons readied and before either had a chance to react, Isabel and Michael were tackled, their arms secured behind their backs.

Three of the intruders were from the council' elite guard, the others from the prefect' security force, both charged with maintaining the separation of heart and mind. Isabel and Michael had known from the beginning that their relationship was taboo but neither was prepared for the feelings each would have for the other. Their attraction was purely physical at first and while coupling between the two races was forbidden, both governments turned a blind eye to it providing it remained just that.

But for Isabel and for Michael, the mental and emotional attraction was instantaneous. There was no denying that they were attracted to each other, Michael was a near perfect male specimen. At just over six foot one, he had broad shoulders, a powerful chest and back. Strong legs, and arms that let you know that you were being held. He had shoulder length brown hair, piercing blue eyes and a gentle smile.

Isabel at five foot three was trim and fit with a lush hourglass figure and legs that could crush a man. Her waist length auburn hair hung like a satin wave about her shoulders, complimenting her deep chocolate brown eyes. What drew Michael to her first and foremost was her smile, it was like a burst of sunlight on a dark and cloudy day.

Disentangling herself from the sheets, she climbed into the shower and washed away the thin sheen of sweat that covered her. She took her time washing her hair and stood under the powerful spray as the conditioner set in. She thought of Michael and found herself incapable of tears, as if they'd been spent or dried up since yesterday. Resigned to her fate, she shut off the water and stepped out of the shower.

Michael stood out on the patio and stared at the rising sun. It was going to be the kind of day that warmed the heart and soothed the soul but for Michael it would do neither. His heart was a dead, withered lump in his chest and his soul had been crushed. His life was without meaning since the morning three weeks prior when they'd been separated. He remembered his inability to help her as she struggled against the council' elite guard. Remembered her cries as she was dragged away, naked and helpless. His hand closed reflexively around the mug of coffee he held and the thick porcelain shattered, the fragments digging into his palm.

Michael reacted by crushing the fragments deeper into his flesh, the pain soothing in its intensity. A momentary diversion to the grief he was feeling. Cursing, he shook his hand out and watched as the wounds pushed out the bits of broken mug and closed seamlessly. Bowing his head he wept silently for what he had lost, for the only woman he'd ever loved fully and as he stood there shoulders shaking, his heart breaking he heard the sound of someone approaching.

He turned his back on the intruder and moved to enter his home when a familiar voice called out to him. "I know how I can help." the woman said cheerfully.

Steeling his nerve Michael responded, "Not now Patience, go away."

"Oh for the love of…whatever, you know me better than that." She said as she climbed the steps.

"How did you find me?" Michael asked as he wiped away the tears.

Patience placed a hand on his shoulder and turned him slowly to face her. "You're famous silly. Everyone's talking about the rogue Arcturian warrior who dared fall in love with the Andromedan princess. Oh and you forgot to mention she was royalty too you know." She said as she brushed past him. "Now go blow your nose and make me a mug of hot chocolate and let me tell you how I can help."

Michael eyed her warily and said softly, "Why do you want to help me?"

Patience looked at Michael with the deepest sympathy and said, "I am Loram Michael. I know what it is to love the impossible. I know the reasons why we rationalize against it. Our hearts fighting our minds when it comes to love and relationships. It's something the prefect and the council lack, the ability to think through love and the courage to accept it in their hearts and blah, blah, blah. Hot chocolate…now!"

Leading her into his home, Michael had to admit that if anyone understood what he was going through it would be a Loram and at this point he had nothing left to loose.

Isabel moved slowly down the stark white corridors towards the room set up for visiting family and friends. She knew that within the four walls sat her mother, sister and a handful of friends. They'd called ahead to let her know that they'd be there waiting for her, waiting to support her and Isabel indeed made them wait. The call had come two and a half hours earlier but despite the insistence of her handlers, she'd taken her sweet time readying herself. She'd dressed, applied her make up then decided to read for a good hour before exiting her room.

Standing outside the door to the family room she listened in on the idle chatter going on within the walls. "She's being petulant…" Her mother was saying loudly. "I think it's romantic…" Her sister mused only to be reprimanded sternly. "Do you want a room next to hers? Do not test me on this young lady. Those of the house of Arcturus are soft, weak." Her mother shouted. "And yet they are the finest of warriors who *WE* hire to protect *US*." Her sister added confidently. "Warriors, please, the one who desecrated your sister, the heir to the throne was nothing more than a mindless sack of worthless emotions. Not worthy to lick our boots let alone what he did to my poor child."

That. Was. The. Last. Straw!

Furious, Isabel stormed into the room, hatred emanating from her pores like a sickly sweat.

She glanced around the room, staring each of them square in the eye sparing only her sister the faintest of smiles. Her mother looked at her flustered and moved to hug her. "No!" Isabel shouted, stopping her mother dead in her tracks. "It is you who are not worthy of licking the boots of the only man I've ever loved." She paused and stepped back towards the door. "To think it was my own mother who betrayed me to the elite guard. To think that her own self importance was worth more than my happiness."

Her mother sat and tried to look contrite but failed miserably. She stood again and paced the small room, "You do realize what would have happened if you'd been joined? You would have lost your soul and been condemned to a Loram' lifetime only to wither with old age and sickness and for what? To die? To give up your immortality? To lay a taint on my house?"

"Your house? *Your* house? Have you forgotten mother," Isabel spat, the word mother a foul thing in her mouth. "Have you forgotten that you were no more than a stray when my father found you? A mongrel? Had my father, *our* father," She said with a nod to Selene, "Had he not looked at you through the eyes of his heart he would have surely have had you put down." The room went dead still and Isabel smiled. "Never forget," She added. "My father's *love* for you saved you, you hateful bitch."

She turned then and opened the door then turned to face her mother for the last time. "Oh how terrible a thing to loose my soul and gain a heart to love with, to be content for the first time in millennia, to love the man I chose to be with and to finally be at rest. Oh yes mother, how horrible a fate." Then looking at her sister she smiled and said, "I love you Selene. See you in a few weeks."

Patience sat across from Michael and sipped from her mug. Michael had an air of brokenness about him that she understood only too well. She'd had her heart broken at an early age when the man she had met and fallen hopelessly in love with died at the hands of his abusive father. Michael had it far worse. Condemned to never see the woman he loved ever again, he was left alone to wander through eternity with the torment of knowing that she would never remember him and that he would never forget her and what they'd shared.

"May I see the ring?" She asked and Michael frowned at her.

"Why?" He asked as he pulled it from his finger.

"I'd like to compare it." Patience asked as she rummaged through her purse and withdrew a small black velvet box. Handing her the ring, Michael watched as she opened the box and removed an exact copy. Inspecting them side by side she smiled and handed Michael the ring from the box.

Michael looked at the engraving and felt tears threatening to spill from his clear blue eyes. The inscription read 'Isabel, always and forever. Michael. I'll be waiting'. "It's beautiful," He said. "But how will this help?"

Patience took the ring and returned it to the box and slipped it into her purse. "Look…" she said as she handed him a card key.

Michael looked at it and his eyes widened. "You have access to the center?" He asked in an awed tone.

Patience sat back and smiled broadly. "I've been a busy little bee since last night. I not only have access to the center but I've been placed on her detail. More to the point, I've been designated her custodian."

Michael' jaw dropped and he struggled to form the words that ran amok in his mind. "Loram' are always used at the center; this way neither the council nor the prefect could have any direct influence."

Michael stood and walked over to the window his thoughts awhirl. "How did you manage to get in though? You told me last night you had no formal training; that you were a free spirit with only a passion for the written word, sex and song."

Patience stood and joined Michael by the window and leaned her head against his shoulder. "I *am* a free spirit Michael," She said softly. "Free to do as she wishes, free to help right a horrible wrong, free to call in a favor or two to do so. So, I did. I start the day after tomorrow."

5

Isabel sat in front of the fireplace and read from a collection of stories that had been left for her. Disgusted with the tome, she threw it into the crackling flames and pulled her feet up under her, wrapping her arms about her knees. The book had been left on her nightstand while she'd been confronting her mother. It was a useless compilation of stories about true love among the Andromedans. Love longed for, love found, love embraced. Love without the benefit of the heart, love bereft of any emotion, love based on mutual respect for the mind.

Love was an emotion of the heart, Michael had taught her that. What the mind couldn't rationalize, the heart embraced while that which the heart couldn't comprehend, the mind explained. Love was not love unless the two embraced. Love was impossible unless the heart and mind became one. The mind allowing for the irrational while the heart made room for the rational.

What the council couldn't wrap their brains around was that it was possible for two people, one from either realm, to fall in love while the prefect refused to accept that the heart and mind could co-exist in peace and harmony. This is what separated their races, what set them apart, both believing that the other was inferior. The council believed that the heart was weak and therefore unreliable while the prefect believed that the mind was devoid of emotion and therefore lacking.

One of the first things Michael had done was take her to Tarkon Park to watch the Loram interact with each other. At first, Isabel noticed the imperfections. The irrational decisions they made while together. Michael patiently pointed out the joy, anger, happiness, frustration and love that each brought to those relationships. Isabel didn't see it but then, all she did see was Michael with his roguish good looks and his innate ability to make even the most puritan of subjects seem erotic in nature.

She was happy with him and try as she might to fight it, his heart won over her mind the first time he looked lovingly into her eyes, the first time he'd caressed her cheek which was incidentally, the first time they'd kissed. She remembered it as if it was yesterday. His mouth claimed hers as he kissed her softly. His tongue branding hers as he deepened the kiss. Before she knew it she'd abandoned all thought and lost herself in his embrace.

Relationships among the people of the house of Andromeda were based on the logical conclusion that two people, somewhat attracted to each other should be joined for the betterment of their race Relationships among the people of the house of Arcturus were encouraged based on emotion alone with little or no regards to the intellectual, financial or familial ramifications. "This is why…" Michael had said, "When the best of both worlds collide it truly is a match made in heaven. Immortality be damned, to live one Loram' lifetime with your perfect mate is far better than living an eternity with someone you are indifferent about."

Isabel had to agree, the two did balanced each other out. While the Arcturians were carefree and could live a life of financial strife, eking out a living paycheck to paycheck, content to be in love; the Andromedans mastery of all things intellectual and financial could make life for the chosen mates that much better.

The Arcturians were happy to love for the sake of loving, believing that 'it would all work out.' Andromedans were fine with being with someone solely because it would increase their stature and position. Both were wrong and the only way to right a wrong was to love because the person you loved was the right one for you. Despite how wrong for each other they were, Michael and Isabel were right for each other in every way.

Michael made up a bed in the guest room and showed Patience where she could shower. He gave her free reign of the house for the night but stopped her outside of his bedroom. "This room is off limits to everyone but my Isabel." He said softly. "If the house is burning down around our ears and this room is the only way out to safety…I'll remember to lay flowers down at your funeral."

Patience leaned against the doorframe and smiled up at Michael. "Wow, forceful, direct and just a tad neurotic don't you think? Listen Mikey, you're attractive and all but you're seriously not my type so if the house does indeed burn down around our ears, I'll be the one vaulting over the bed to safety. You're welcome to try to catch up."

Michael exhaled slowly and looked down at Patience. "Mikey? Really?" He asked and was rewarded with a dazzling smile. "Look, I'm sorry Patience," He said and kissed her forehead. "I'm a wreck and the fact that you are willing to put yourself in harms way for Isabel and I...well...I can't express my gratitude adequately. I'm sorry if I sounded harsh, it's just that you are Loram and well..."

"And well..." Patience said with a smile. "I told you I'm a free spirit Mikey, not a whore. Loram' have a bad rep that way which is why I live the way I do. Free from the stereotype, free to do as I please. You have nothing to worry about. I'm in it for love."

Michael bid Patience good night and watched as she entered the guest room, closing the door behind her. He went back downstairs and into the kitchen. Pouring himself a glass of Scotch, he took his time closing up the house for the night. Satisfied that everything was secured he slowly made his way back up the stairs and locked himself in his bedroom.

Placing the scotch on the night table he undressed, hung up his clothes and crawled into bed. He leaned back against the headboard and ran his fingers through his hair, massaging his scalp. His thoughts began to race, one tumbling over the other as he thought of his Isabel, of his long, eternal life without her, of the risk Patience was taking. Thought after thought came crashing down one on top of the other and heart aching, he rolled over to her side of the bed and buried his face in her pillow, inhaling her scent. He choked back a sob as the first wave of grief washed over him then gave into the tears. He'd never loved anyone as he did Isabel. She was his perfect match the yin to his yang, the light to his dark. Growing up he'd always believed that true love was found in the arms of your hearts equal and that he would one day marry an Arcturian. Now he knew that true love knew no boundaries, that it transcended both realms.

He would give his very life for her, battle any demon. His life was meaningless without her smile, her touch, her very being. Michael allowed his mind to wander back to the first time they'd met. Back to that day eons ago when they were sequestered in a room to finalize the papers for a transfer of realm to the Loram. He was immediately struck by her presence, at five foot three she was packaged in such a way that had him hardening every time he glanced her way.

Her legs were strong and shapely, her hips and waist the perfectly proportioned frame for her little heart shaped ass. Her stomach wasn't flat but she was a woman who cared about her figure. Her tear drop breasts, were captured by the black lace corset she wore. Her face, framed by the long auburn hair was angelic with freckles sprinkled liberally about her cheeks, and her smile; her smile was the killer. That smile of hers cast the sun into shadow.

Physical attraction aside it was her spirit that captured his heart as she argued the finer details of the agreement. This woman had more passion than anyone he had ever met. They agreed to disagree and decided to finish up their work over a dinner brought in by a local Loram catering company. They dined on shrimp and pasta drank a decent Sauvignon Blanc and chatted idly about nothing in particular. Finally, after a bottle and a half of the wine Isabel looked up at him and smiled. Her hand reached across the table and took his, "I like you Michael," She said softly…seductively. "We work well together."

Michael shifted uncomfortably in his seat trying to discreetly shift his growing erection. "I like you too Isabel," He replied. "I think we'd do anything well together." Isabel smiled at him wickedly and pulled her hand back. Leaning back against her chair she stretched and looked at him under her thick canopy of lashes. "Anything?" She said quietly. Michael struggled to tear his gaze away from the soft round mounds that spilled from the top of her corset and licked his lips. "Anything..." He said and stood slowly.

Isabel watched as he approached her, his erection trapped between his black leather pants and his leg. Michael took her hand and drew her to her feet slowly, appreciating every subtle movement of her body. "Care to dance?" He said and she smiled at him. "There's no music." She responded as he pulled her into him. She placed her head against his chest as he wrapped strong arms around her, her hands caressing his back. "You can dance to what you hear my heart singing to you, dance to the way you make me feel, dance to what you're doing to me right now. Dance to what you will... but dance." He said.

And dance they did.

6

Isabel fell asleep in front of the fireplace wrapped in a blanket and thought of everything Michael was to her determined to capture and hold onto every memory. She remembered their first dance in a boardroom in the wee hours of the morning. She remembered how his heart thrummed in his chest. She remembered how he moved with her, sinuously, sensually. His hard muscular body felt so good pressed against hers. She remembered the moment his lips brushed against hers, soft but insistent.

She had melted in his embrace, heart racing as she kissed him with a passion she'd never felt before. It was as if they were one mind one body one soul. She wanted him then and without a thought, she cast away all inhibitions and pulled him towards the conference room table. He had picked her up half way there and laid her on her back. Like two animals in heat they'd torn at the others clothing, desperate for flesh to touch flesh. Her corset had been stripped away as his hand worked up her skirt to remove the panties that weren't there. Michael growled deep in his throat and laved her nipples with his tongue as he plundered her wet aching core with first one finger, then another. Her breasts were swollen with desire, her nipples hard points that scraped his chest as he leaned into her and teased her ear and the tender flesh of her neck.

Isabel worked his pants down to his knees, freeing him. She took him in her small hand and stroked him as he sucked, licked and nibbled her tender flesh. Laying back she slid her ass towards the edge of the table and rubbed his cock against her tight wet opening. "Inside me...I want you inside me baby." She purred and taking her by the hips, Michael slowly entered her inch by glorious inch.

Patience slept fitfully, her dreams scattered and vivid. Never having been able to remember them once she awoke, she trained herself to wake up, jot them down and fall immediately back to sleep. She believed that once she had everything down on paper, she'd be able to make sense of the fleeting images and emotions. At the very least she'd have the workings of a twisted and compelling novel. It was a quarter past three in the morning when she awoke in a feverish sweat.

Michael was dead…so was Isabel and Patience found herself before the council and the prefect. There was a trial going on and many of the members were screaming and shouting; hurling barbs and epitaphs at each other. Patience stood in the middle of the circular room and turned slowly, arms outstretched in supplication. "Please!" She shouted over the din. "Please listen to me; you all need to hear this." The roaring of the crowds grew louder and louder and falling to her knees, Patience sobbed into her hands.

She set the paper and the pen aside and curled up into the fetal position wondering what she had gotten herself into. She believed that two people destined for each other should be allowed the opportunity to love and be loved but at what cost? Could the love Michael and Isabel shared bring about war? Bring about the destruction of everything the Andromedans and the Arcturians had fought so long to uphold?   As Loram she had a part to play in keeping the peace between the realms and it was a part she did not take lightly.

Michael and Isabel deserved a shot and maybe her part would be in keeping the peace despite the consequences. Maybe she had a bigger role to play in the grand scheme of things, maybe she could bridge the gap between the realms and see an age where people both mortal and immortal lived and loved freely. That was a lot of maybe's. Perhaps more maybes than one lone Loram could handle…maybe. Sleep finally overcame her and patience dreamt no more only to be awakened at six am to the sounds and smells of breakfast cooking.

Patience showered and dressed, securing her long flowing blond hair in a tight ponytail. Descending the stairs, she found Michael in the kitchen hard at work. On the table was a feast fit for a king. He had made omelets, crepes, bacon and sausage, whole wheat and sourdough toast and several jars of jam, coffee and tea. Michael turned and smiled at her, it was a sad and tired smile. Evidently he didn't sleep any better then she had.

Pointing at a chair with the spatula he held he said simply, "Sit. Eat."

Patience did as she was told and stared at the spread. "This is…" She began and Michael laughed.

"Overwhelming I know; I wasn't sure what you wanted for breakfast and I like to cook so…"

Patience began loading a plate and laughed. "I'm used to a bowl of corn flakes and a hot chocolate." She said then added, "But this is magnificent." Michael smiled and placed a steaming mug of hot chocolate before her and next to it, a box of corn flakes.

"Now you're showing off." Patience said and sighed as she bit into one of the strawberry banana crepes. "This is divine." She said as she followed the crepes with a swallow of hot chocolate and a mouthful of the three cheese omelet. "This is…" She said as she poked at the omelet with her fork.

"Asiago, aged cheddar and jack cheese." He supplied and Patience closed her eyes, savoring the flavors. "I might never leave." She said and smiled at him as he sat down opposite her.

Michael tucked into the elaborate breakfast and ate silently for awhile before clearing his throat and asking the one question that had been burning in his heart since the night before. "When do you leave?" He said cautiously and watched as Patience laid her fork down next to her plate. "In the morning, I have to be at the processing center by eight thirty."

Michael nodded and returned to eating. Patience watched him quietly and finally said with an air of confidence she didn't feel, "It's going to work Michael. The ring's already in place, with someone I trust. I'll help her to remember, I promise you I will."

Michael felt the knot in his gut tighten slightly and stared at his food. Then with a look that implied he'd been taken for a fool, he glared at Patience. "LIAR!" He roared and she recoiled. "You have the ring! You showed it to me not twelve hours ago!"

Patience went from frightened to aghast to bemused in the time it took Michael to swallow the lump that had formed in his throat. "Why are you smiling?" He asked menacingly.

"You are such a knob!" Patience laughed, reaching into the pocket of her robe. She withdrew a small black box identical to the one she'd shown him the day before and slid it across the table. Michael looked at it as if it would detonate as soon as he touched it.

"Open it douche wad." Patience said with a laugh.

"Douche wad?" Michael said as he cupped the box. "Lovely, you kiss many people with that mouth?"

"Open it." She said with mounting frustration and Michael did. Inside was an exact duplicate of the ring she'd shown him only the inscription read, *'Michael, I will remember. Wait for me. Isabel.'*

Before he could speak, Patience said. "I ran home to get my bag yesterday yes?" Michael nodded, shame biting at him. "I dropped off the ring with another Loram also working her detail. He's more militant but entirely trustworthy. He'd do anything to stick it to the Andromedans and the Arcturians."

"I'm sorry." Michael said in a voice so quiet, Patience almost wanted to ask him to repeat himself. Instead, she smiled and nodded.

"No biggie…douche wad."

They finished their breakfast in relative silence and Michael offered to take her shopping for anything she may need for the trip to the center. Patience while reluctant at first took him up on his offer after a brief but heated exchange. Both on edge, they left the house in Michaels century mark four and drove to the cities busiest mall. They had agreed to play the part of the immortal and his Loram concubine for the sake of keeping people from staring and looping her arm about his, which seemed to be becoming a habit, they entered the bustling mall.

Four and a half hours later, Michael and Patience left the shops, their arms laden with assorted bags. "And you are absolutely positive you need all these things?" He asked with a laugh. "You were quite adamant before we left that you didn't need anything."

Patience cast her eyes downward and said softly, "My sister doesn't have much since her husband left her, I've wanted to get her a few things I'm sorry Michael; let's just bring them back ok?" Patience turned abruptly and headed back towards the mall.

Michael stopped her and turned her to face him. "There is no way I can repay you for what you are about to do for me…for Isabel. Tell me what she needs and I will provide it."

Patience wiped away the tears that started to collect on her heavy lashes and smiled. "Isabel is a very lucky woman Michael, I envy her."

Michael wiped away an errant tear that had fallen onto Patience' cheek and smiled at her. "The way I see it, Isabel and I are the lucky ones; we would never have had a chance if you hadn't stalked me in the park, you are a part of our family now. For you we would do anything."

Patience punched him in the arm and laughed. "No more mushy stuff today buddy. I might just start liking you. Now take me to my sisters place, I'd like you to meet her."

7

Isabel showered and dressed in the white pantsuit that had been laid out for her. It felt like pulling on a burial shroud and in essence, that was exactly what she was doing, dressing for her funeral. In a matter of hours, the council would be laying to rest every memory of Michael she had. She ate sparingly and sat on the bed, too wound up to relax before the procedure. She thought of Michael, she thought of the procedure and she thought about what her life would be like without any memory of him.

Two hours before they would be coming for her, there was a soft knock on the door. Before she could do anything, the door opened and her sister poked her head in. "Selene!" Isabel cried as she sprang from the bed. The two women collided in the middle of the room and hugged each other as the tears flowed. "What are you d-d-doing here?" Isabel said through the sobs and Selene pulled her towards the sofa.

"I wanted to see you before they came." Selene said as she pulled a strip of paper out of her boot. "I wanted to give you this…" Isabel took the paper and read what her sister had written on it. The note read, 'Remember Michael Isabel. Never forget Michael.'

Isabel read and re-read the note scrawled in her sisters flowing script and hugged her again. "How did you get this in here?" She asked quietly and Selene smiled.

"I'm dating one of the guards…at least until this is all over…maybe?"

Isabel laughed, clamping her hand over her mouth to stifle the sound. "You little tramp!" She cried. "I love you!"

Selene just smiled and shrugged her shoulders. "He's not bad really, a little younger but he's in great shape and kinda funny in a geeky sorta way."

"You're a heartbreaker sis," Isabel said as she tucked the note away in the folds of her pantsuit.

"Meh…" Selene said offhandedly. "What's one heart broken for two restored?"

Selene kept Isabel company for the better part of an hour then when a soft knock on the door interrupted them, Selene stood. "I have to go Izzy that was my cue."

Isabel stood, her stomach clenched painfully. "I wish you could stay for a little while longer."

Selene hugged her sister and kissed her on the cheek. "I'll see you in a few weeks sweetie. Be strong." Isabel nodded and watched as her sister slipped from the room.

Michael drove into the seediest part of any town he'd ever visited. How the Loram lived like this he would never understand. The ramshackle buildings and tenements reeked of despair yet all along the side streets children played and couples walked hand in hand oblivious to their situation. They parked in front of a three storey apartment complex and Patience got out of the car. Michael followed hesitantly, bags in hand and followed her up the front steps.

Surprisingly, the interior of the building was clean and painted a vibrant rainbow of colors. Michael followed Patience up the stairs to the second floor and waited to the side as she knocked on the door to apartment two seventeen. Moments later the door opened and a woman slightly shorter than Patience swung it open. "I told you I'd have the rent by…" The woman said stopping short at the sight of her sister. "Patience? What on earth are you doing here?" the woman said as two children between the ages of four and eight pushed their way past her.

"Auntie Patience!" They cried in unison as they each latched onto and hugged her legs.

Patience staggered under their weight and tousled their hair. "Hey guys." She said and smiling up at her sister added, "Can we come in?"

The woman eyed Michael for a long time and shrugged. "I thought you'd told me you'd sworn off of anything remotely Arcturian sis." The woman said as she stepped aside and ushered them in.

Patience kissed her sisters cheek as she passed her and said, "Michael this is my sister Serenity; Serenity…Michael."

Michael placed the bags down on the coffee table and turned. "Pleased to meet you Serenity." He said as he shook her hand.

Patience' sister blushed every shade of red at the deep rumbling sound of Michael' voice. "Oh Patience; keep this one." She stage whispered. "That or just leave him here, I promise to take very good care of him."

Patience laughed and began unpacking the bags. "These are for you and the kids." She said and handed each of the kids a pile of clothing.

"Patience what is this? It's not like you're rolling in dough." Serenity said and put down the clothing that she had handed her.

"I've got a job so I'll be gone for a few weeks, maybe longer. Michael has offered to watch out for you while I'm gone."

Serenity watched the two warily and folded her arms across her chest. "What kind of job?" Then turning to Michael said, "Just what is it you've got my sister doing for you buddy?"

Michael slid next to Patience and kissed her cheek. "It is not I that has her doing anything Serenity, this I assure you. What Patience is doing she is doing of her own free will and from the depths of a heart that humbles me."

Patience beamed at him and waggled her eyebrows at her sister. Michael glanced at his watch and said, "May I be excused?" As the two women stared at each other.

"Sure…" Patience said never taking her eyes off of her sister. "We'll be right here waiting for our eyes to dry out." Serenity snorted and blinked first which made Patience shoot her arms up over her head as she danced a little victory dance. "Hurry up though ok?" She said as Michael walked to the door. "My sister's about to make her homemade, never to be equaled, kick ass hot chocolate for us; aren't you sis?"

Isabel was being walked between two of the Loram who were armed to the teeth. They walked down a sterile white corridor towards the end of the complex in silence. "In here." The shorter of the two said, gesturing towards a door on the left. Isabel waited as the man opened the door and ushered her in. She waited as the second man opened a door on the far left wall and flipped on a series of switches. The room was instantly bathed in a sickly green light and Isabel noticed a wall made entirely of mirror. "Wait until were inside then strip down; everything goes in the incinerator." He said the last pointing at a hole no bigger than one foot in diameter to the left of the door they'd entered.

Isabel felt her heart drop down into her stomach and sighed. All the risks her sister had taken, the note, her only chance at remembering and it was all about to go up in a puff of smoke…literally. She nodded and waited for the two men to enclose themselves in behind the two way mirrored walls. She closed her eyes and waited; her heartbeat loud in her ears. "Any time now miss." A voice said over the tinny speaker in the ceiling.

Angry now, Isabel stripped down quickly and wadding up the strip of paper in with the clothes, stuffed them into the incinerator. "There; happy..? Get a good look?" She said through clenched teeth. A moment passed and the door the two men had disappeared behind opened.

The second man, taller and better looking than the first came over to her cautiously. "Miss…" He said careful to keep his eyes on hers and no where else. "I am Loram and while I have a job to do; I don't have to like it. I believe that everyone should be able to choose who to love but as Loram; I have no say in the matters of neither the Andromedan Council nor the Arcturian Prefect."

Isabel cast her eyes downward and stared at her feet. "I know…" She said as her tears flowed freely. "I miss him."

The man reached out and took her hand gently. "I'll stay with you, you won't be alone." Nodding, Isabel allowed him to lead her out the door and down the corridor to the room on the end. The room that would undo centuries of happiness and love.

"So that wasn't the room then." Isabel stated.

"No," The Loram said shaking his head. "That was the scanner room. Scans you for memorabilia if you will. Ensures a clean wipe."

Isabel stared at her feet as they walked the corridor. "Oh." She whispered, the only word her constricting throat could manage.

Michael took the stairs back down to the foyer and pulled his phone from his pocket. He dialed quickly and listened as the phone rang, "I didn't think I'd be hearing from you this quick." The voice on the other end said gruffly and Michael winced. He hated calling his brother who was instrumental in his being sentenced to this little corner of hell but the alternative had been far worse so for that he was grateful.

"Bryce," Michael said with just a hint of warning in his voice. "Bryce, please. I need a favor."

The silence on the other end was interminable and for a second Michael expected to hear a dial tone. Instead his brother sighed and said, "I'm sorry Michael, what is it that you need?"

Dispensing with niceties he got straight to the point. "The place; the big one over by Fulcrum Point...the three bedrooms, two baths, is that up for sale still? I remember you telling me about it a few months ago, said it was the perfect place for someone like me."

Bryce chuckled and coughed into his hand. "Oh yeah it's still up for sale. At the price they're asking it will be for centuries."

"Buy it." Michael said cutting his brother off mid sentence. "Outfit one room for a girl, one for a boy both under the age of ten and finish off the third for a woman in her thirties."

"Umm Michael," Bryce said suspiciously.

"Do it Bryce; please. Spare no expense and make sure there's clothing and toys...lots of toys. I'll take care of the necessities for the mother." There was another long silence in which both brothers were choosing their words very carefully.

Michael was the first to break the silence. "Listen Bryce," He said. "I'm stuck here without hope of shifting anywhere and I'd like to help this struggling mother of two. If my life is to be without meaning I at least want to make sure that hers isn't."

Bryce paused long enough to make sure that Michael was finished then said, "Ok Michael, I'll do it but this is going to cost you a ton of credits."

Michael laughed and said, "That's fine; I have twenty tons of credits so it shouldn't hurt much. What's the address?" Bryce gave it to him and saying their goodbyes, Michael hung up feeling better about things than he had in weeks.

Just then, the wind died down and the silence that descended over the city was chilling. It held a sense of foreboding. Like the city had been gagged, like it was holding its breath. Just then, the clock tower in the square chimed. Twelve resounding gongs that was heard from one end of the city to the other. His heart fell and tears unbidden seeped from his closed eyelids as he leaned against the railing that led up to the door to Serenity's building. Isabel' punishment was being exacted out right at twelve o'clock...their time was up.

Isabel was led into a room much like the one she'd been staying in. There was a fireplace offset in the corner and a fire was casting dancing shadows against the dark umber walls. the heat from the fire warmed her chilled flesh, caressing her like a lover. The bed was similar to hers except that it was clinical in its sterility. Crisp white linens and hospital grade blankets covered it. The nightstand on one side of the bed was decorated with flowers and a portrait of her and her family. A glass of water and a pitcher on the other. Isabel felt instantly drowsy and she yawned.

"What's that smell?" She asked sleepily as the technician led her to the bed.

"It's sleep," The technician said softly as he drew back the blankets for her. "When you wake up it will be a brand new day miss." He said as Isabel got nestled into bed.

"Isabel," She said sleepily. "My names Isabel."

The technician tucked the blankets about her tiny five foot two inch frame and bent low to whisper in her ear. "My names Michael Isabel. Remember Michael and I'll be right here when you wake up." Isabel smiled sleepily as she was drawn down into the yawning abyss of REM sleep.

She stood with her back to the precipice and braced herself on two unsteady legs as every memory of...of...oh hell she couldn't remember what it was she was forgetting. 'It mustn't have been all that important' she mused to herself as the last of the memories dropped off the precipice and into an endless void. Standing there, she considered joining her memories, of launching herself into the void but couldn't bring herself to do it. Yawning, she stretched and slowly, sparing only a casual glance backwards walked away from the edge.

As promised, the intern or orderly or whatever he was, was there when she awoke after what he had informed her was a thirteen minute sleep. She glanced at him and smiled then the sound of movement in the corner pulled her attention away. "Good morning Isabel." Her mother said coolly.

"Fuck!" Isabel said and turned to the young man. "I'm still asleep and in the middle of a nightmare aren't I?"

The young man tried as hard as he could to suppress a smile but failed miserably. "'I'm afraid not." He laughed then stretched. "I have to go back to work but I'll check in on you later if that's ok?"

"That is most definitely NOT ok." Isabel' mother snapped. "You've done your job Loram. Leave now and you won't loose it."

"She's a grumpy old bag isn't she?" He said and it was Isabel' turn to smile.

"Take her with you," She said quietly. "If you can, send for my sister Selene."

The young man smiled and nodded. "Of course," He said then standing, pointed at Isabel' mother. "You. With me." He said with just a hint of warning in his tone.

Isabel' mother faltered a bit then followed him out of the room without so much as a sideways glance in Isabel' direction. "If we were in *my* realm..." She heard her mother say.

"But you're not grumpy. Let's go." She heard the intern retort as the door closed. For the first time in what seemed like forever, Isabel smiled.

Michael steadied his emotions and mounted the stairs slowly. He had to believe that Patience would be able to jog Isabel' memory. An immortal lifetime without anything but his memories would crush him under their weight and he shuddered to think of what he'd become if that was his fate. He knew deep within his soul that he would be incapable of loving another yet equally so, he couldn't imagine a lifetime of loneliness.

He knocked on the door to Serenity' apartment and entered at the sound of both Isabel and Charity shouting for him to 'come in'. The kids were sitting at the dilapidated coffee table furiously coloring in the new coloring books Patience had bought them while Patience and Charity sat at the kitchen table. "You look like ass." Patience said and instantly regretted it. The haunted look in Michael's eyes meant one thing and one thing only. Isabel was lost to him.

"Oh I am so sorry Michael." She offered as she stood and wrapped her arms around him. "Being around my sister brings out the 'special ed' in me." Michael returned the hug and sat wearily at the table. Pulling a card from his pocket, he handed it to Serenity.

"What's this?" She asked as she read the address. "It is for you and your children." He replied without making eye contact.

Patience took the card and read it. "Michael you didn't!" She exclaimed happily.

"Didn't what?" Serenity asked.

"Guilty as charged." Michael said with the faintest hint of a smile. "Give them a week and I'll send someone to collect you and your possessions."

"I beg your pardon?" Serenity said in a whisper.

"Michael just bought you the house on Fulcrum Point." Patience said and Serenity' jaw dropped.

"*The* house?" She asked, glancing from Patience to Michael and back again.

"Yeah..." Michael said quietly and both women screeched in delight.

Once the two women had calmed down, Serenity turned and faced Michael tears brimming in her eyes. "Why Michael? Why do this for me and my children?"

Michael' gaze was piercing, filled with heat and anger, remorse and a deep and abiding love. When he spoke his voice was low and it sounded like water over gravel. "What I did, I did for Patience. She has taught me; an Arcturian no less; what it is to love without question, without guilt or remorse. What she has offered to do for me I can never repay so I did what I could but my debt is far from settled."

"Michael," Patience said as she took his hand gently. "There is no guarantee that any of this will work, no guarantee that I will succeed."

Michael straightened in his seat and fixed that stoic gaze on Patience. "The fact that you offered is enough to have made up my mind. You and your sister will never lack for anything; ever. You..." He said pointing at Serenity. "Will know peace and security, your children will know happiness and you..." He said returning his gaze to Patience. "You will have anything and everything you have ever desired. Ask and it will be given you; to both of you."

Serenity sat back and studied her children in the other room. "I want to know exactly what it is you're going to do Patience. I need to know you're not going to do something stupid."

Isabel waited for the better part of the morning and still her sister hadn't come. All kind of terrible images swam through her thoughts, none of which made any sense. The intern had poked his head in on two occasions to see how she was doing but with every passing hour, Isabel sank deeper and deeper into a funk.

Stomach rumbling, Isabel showered quickly in the event her sister would show and she picked up the phone on the desk next to the door which was locked from the outside. After trying the knob, Isabel swallowed her growing panic and misdialed the number for the center' cafeteria twice before getting it right. Reading from the list of instructions next to the phone, she ordered a lunch better suited for a family and sat back down in the chair besides the fireplace and waited.

Finally, after what seemed like an eternity, her door opened and a sprite of a woman pushed a cart inside. "You must be hungry," She said cheerfully, her eyes bright and her smile picture perfect. "I can't remember the last time someone ordered this much food."

Isabel smiled at the woman and sighed, "Yeah, I'm hungry all right. Can you tell me if my sister's on her way?"

The woman peered at Isabel and nodded. "Yup, well, no…I can't but I know someone who can. I'll have Miles come up to see you in a bit." Isabel nodded and watched as the woman stepped out of the room with a little wave.

Why the hell are all the Loram so damned cheerful all the time? She wondered to herself. Isabel felt as if she'd gone to sleep and had woken up missing the better part of herself. Inside her there was a deep and fathomless void she couldn't fill. Something was missing, niggling at the outer recesses of her mind just out of her reach and it troubled her deeply.

She was just finishing off a Greek salad when a soft knock drew her attention towards the door. "I believe you've been looking for someone?" A tall, bald headed man with the skin the color of dark rich coffee said as he pushed the door open wide. Behind him stood her sister Selene with a massive bouquet of flowers in hand and sporting a wicked bruise under her left eye.

Isabel was at once ecstatic and mortified. "Selene?" She whispered as her sister walked gingerly into the room, favoring her right leg and her ribs.

"Hey sis." Selene said softly. It was then that Isabel noticed her lip was split. Propelling herself out of the chair she took the flowers from Selene and tossed them onto the bed. Guiding her sister to the love seat beside the fire, Isabel lowered her into it gently and sat next to her, eyes wide.

Before Isabel could launch the first of a hundred questions at her, Selene raised her hand and motioned for her to wait. After a few shallow breaths, Selene smiled as best she could and said, "This is all worth it if it worked." She said simply and Isabel furrowed her brow.

"If what worked sweetie?" She asked, taking Selene' hand. "The note; Michael. Please god, tell me you remember." Selene said, panic constricting her chest.

Isabel raised her hand and stroked her sister' cheek. "Who's Michael?" She asked as the first of Selene' tears spilled from her dark obsidian eyes.

9

Michael drove Patience back to his place after she had managed to somewhat convince her sister that she wasn't going on a suicide mission. They prepared a light supper and sat in silence as they ate. The visit with her sister Serenity had overwhelmed Michael and filled him with equal parts hope and despair.   Once they had returned to Michael's home, a pall had settled on him like a cloak. "It's done you know." He said as he pushed his food around on his plate.

Patience sat, uncertain as to how to respond. Finally she said quietly, "Yes; I know. But it isn't over Michael. This is just the beginning.

Pushing away from the table, Michael stalked over to the kitchen and returned with a bottle of eight year old Sahale brandy and two glasses.

"None for me Michael. They won't let me into the processing center with alcohol in my system. I have to be at least twenty-four hours."

"Right, forgot." Michael said as he twisted the cap off and drank straight from the bottle. Patience eyed him warily and pointed at the glasses. "What are those for?"

"Thought I'd be civilized; you're not joining me so fuck it."

"Ah," She replied. "Gotcha. Given up already eh?" The words were out of her mouth so fast she flinched.

"Yes...no...what the fuck do you want from me!" He exploded. "Everything I've ever loved was taken from me today, everything I've ever cared for, fought for...would die for! I can't, I can't..." Michael sank to the floor his body wracked with the most heart wrenching sobs Patience had ever heard.

"Michael," She said as she stood and settled onto the floor next to him, holding him. "Michael, it'll be ok, I promise...you have my word." Michael never heard her, as his sobs reverberated throughout the main floor of the house. It was Patience who, twenty minutes later stood and answered the door.

Isabel's jaw dropped at her sister's reaction to the simple response to her question. "Selene? What is it baby?" She asked quietly as she held her. "What did I say? I just don't know who it is you're asking me about."

Selene wiped at her eyes angrily and sniffing loudly turned to face her sister. "Michael, Isabel; Michael!" She shouted. "You've been together for almost four centuries; FOUR! You're telling me you don't remember a goddamned thing? None of it?"

Isabel sat back, eyeing her sister and slowly shook her head. "I don't, I really don't. But I should shouldn't I?"

"Yeah, you should. He was everything to you. Your reason for getting up in the morning, the air you breathed, your whole world."

Isabel sat for a long time and thought furiously. Nothing. Not one smidge of remembrance at all. No recognition of the name or anything else her sister had said. "I'm sorry baby; I'm drawing a blank." She said finally and shrank back in her seat. "What happened to you? Your face, ribs, leg?"

"Small price to pay when I thought my note would help you remember; now it just seems like a waste."

"Who beat you?" Isabel said, dreading the answer.

"Who else?" Selene said through clenched teeth. "Mom did."

Isabel exploded out of the chair as if she had been strapped to a rocket. "I'll kill the bitch!" She screamed which earned them an "Everything ok in there" from the other side of the door. Crossing the room, Isabel almost wrenched the door off its hinges before the Loram on the other side unbolted it. "Get me my mother." She said then added. "Better yet, just bring me her fucking head."

The Loram smiled at her sweetly and said, "As much as I'd love to, cause let's face it the woman's a bitch, but I like my job." Growling in frustration, Isabel slammed the door in his face and stalked back to her sister.

"Here's my card," She said as she pulled it from her bag on the dresser. "There are enough credits to get you to that cozy little Loram world. What's it called again?"

"Scandia." Selene replied, her voice barely above a whisper.

"Go there Selene, go and get better, heal. Just get away from mom ok?" Selene held out her hand, fingers trembling and took the card.

"I'm sorry Isabel, sorry I failed you." She whispered as she struggled to stand.

Isabel stood and helped her sister up. "There's a café there, on the west side." She said as she moved with her sister to the door. "Opposite a park, best hot chocolate in the world."

Selene stared at her sister for a long moment and said, "And you know this because?" Shrugging her shoulders Isabel said with a faltering smile. "I dunno, I just do."

Bryce filled the doorway the way Michael would have but with more arrogance. "I suppose you're the one Michael has to sign these papers for?" He said, raking Patience with a scathing glare.

Michael, eyes rimmed red, pushed Patience aside gently and took the papers from his brother' hand. He rifled through them, signing where he needed to and handing them to Patience mumbled, "Excuse me." She nodded and with a speed that seemed inhuman, Michael launched himself at his brother, his fist driving the man's head backwards. Blood exploded from where his brother' nose had been. Bryce, despite his size couldn't match Michael blow for blow.

After what seemed like seconds, Michael stood over his brother and pointed down at him. "You!" He roared. "You turned us in, sentenced me to a lifetime of torment and heartache, and sentenced her to a barbaric procedure! You are dead to me. Never set foot on my doorstep again and so help me, if I ever see you within fifty feet of Patience or her family, you will wish you were dead." The words came out with a fury and a savageness that was a palpable thing. They hung in the air like a curse, settling on his brother like a fog.

Bryce looked up at his brother through two swollen eyes, his cheek and nose broken. All of which were healing right before their eyes. He grinned a bloody grin, displaying a set of broken and jagged teeth. "Don't you worry Michael; you'll never see me or our family again. Mark my words; your punishment has only just begun." Michael kicked his brother in the side and Patience heard the ribs snap like kindling. Struggling to his feet, Bryce staggered a little then turned his back on the two of them and without a word, shuffled away.

"Michael, that..." Patience said, stumbling over her thoughts.

"Felt good." Michael said coldly. "I need a drink."

Isabel paced the small quarters, waiting for the Loram to return with her mother, her mind working furiously. *Why do I remember the little café?* She wondered to herself. *Why can't I remember this Michael that's upset Selene so? How could I forget someone I supposedly loved for four centuries?* She ran her trembling fingers through her hair and sighed. Anger at what Selene had had done to her at her mother's hands fueled the rage burning inside her. Her mother, like all Andromedans couldn't die but she would pay dearly for what she'd done to Selene.

Just as the four walls were closing in on her, the door opened and her mother entered, a plastered on grin on her face. "Oh baby, I knew you'd want to see…"

Her words were cut off as Isabel swung and laid a slap across her face that would leave an angry red welt for days. Horrified, her mother spun around from the impact and fell over the loveseat. "You cruel, manipulative bitch!" Isabel screamed as she rounded on her mother. "What you did to Selene; what you did to her is…is… reprehensible!"

Her mother, scrambled around the loveseat, placing it between her and her enraged daughter. "Isabel, listen…" She said.

"No. You listen." Isabel growled, ice and fire glazing her words. "I am done with you, with this family…with everyone but Selene. Consider my role on the council terminated."

"Terminated?" Her mother gasped. "You're the heir, it will ruin us."

"Good, then consider yourself as ruined as that shriveled, blackened lump you call your heart."

"Isabel, be reasonable. Think this through, you're an Andromedan for the love of all things holy."

"Reasonable?" Isabel spat as she lashed out and grabbed her mother's arm in a vise like grip. "Reasonable? Was it reasonable to break Selene's ribs? To blacken her eyes? To split her lips or kick her hard enough to cause her to limp like an old woman?"

"You're the only heir," Her mother wailed as she was dragged to the door. "You're the last, the only hope for our family to continue on with dignity."

"Fuck your dignity, fuck the family and fuck you mom. I never want to see you again." Then turning to the Loram who was having a devil of a time suppressing his grin said, "Toss her down the garbage chute and allow no one but Selene access to me while I am here."

The Loram, much to his credit only nodded his response and taking Isabel' mother by the arm, led her away.

Isabel closed the door and locked it which seemed redundant considering it was locked from the outside as well. Tomorrow she'd be going to the processing center, tomorrow would be a new day, and a new opportunity to change what had become a nightmarish life. Tomorrow. Isabel sighed as her head pounded. She shuffled to the bed and laid down on it. Pulling the pillow over her head she screamed into the mattress. Not surprisingly, it did nothing for her. "Who are you Michael? Why are you important to me? Why can't I remember you?"

10

Patience considered dragging Michael's heavy ass to his bedroom after he'd passed out but remembered his warning about entering his room. Instead she pulled one of the blankets off of her bed and draped it over him on the sofa. Lowering the lights, she turned off the television and kissed him lightly on the cheek.

Padding through the house, she doused the lights and slipped silently into her room. She'd packed her bag earlier in the evening but opened it to make sure she hadn't forgotten anything. Satisfied that she had everything she needed, she tucked the access card and security clearance pass into the thin plastic housing on the end of her lanyard.

Tucking herself into bed, she listened to the silence of the house. Patience was never comfortable with silences, she preferred noise; bustling, chaotic noise. That's what lulled her to sleep, what comforted her in the lonely hours of the night. If there be noise, there be people and if there be people; Patience wasn't alone. She pulled the blanket up under her chin and smiled as Michael's snoring wafted in through the walls.

She'd have to remember to call him 'locomotive breath' tomorrow; borrowing the term from a millennia old Jethro Tull song she'd heard her father sing as he worked on the house they'd lived in. Her heart clenched at the memory of loosing him, of the turmoil her life had become since. Tomorrow would bring more than its share of turmoil. Tomorrow could wait. Michael snored louder and she stifled a giggle. Smiling, she slipped into a deep and surprisingly dreamless sleep; the first in eons.

Morning came far too quickly, the sounds of the city wakening, the sunlight streaming through the window, the smell of burnt coffee. *Burnt coffee?* Michael thought as his stomach lurched. *Oh gods did I really drink an entire bottle of Sahale brandy?* He stood by way of rolling off the sofa, onto his hands and knees, using the table for support, sitting back onto the sofa and lurching to his feet. The room swam sickeningly and he took painfully slow, faltering steps towards the bathroom.

Passing the kitchen, he spied the clock out of the corner of his eye and froze. *That can't be right.* He thought as he forced his eyes to adjust, to clear his thrumming head. Eleven fifty. Three hours and twenty minutes since Patience had to be at the shelter. "Fuck!" He cried as he tore down the hallway to her bedroom. "Patience!" He cried as he rounded the corner, shoulder smashing into the doorframe. "Patience we're…" The words dried up in his throat as he saw her perfectly made bed and the note pinned to the pillow. He entered the room and with trembling fingers took the note, written on his stationary and began to read.

'Michael, I didn't want to wake you. Last night was hard on you and I (selfishly) feared that having to say goodbye to you would have proved to be more than I could bear. Thank you for everything you've done for my sister. The gifts, the security and the house. Thank you for everything you've done for me. You've given me purpose, gave my life meaning and the most precious of all; you've given me something I've never truly had…friendship. You are a good man Michael, Isabel is lucky to have you. I will do everything in my power to see the two of you together again. With all my love. Patience.'

Michael sat heavily on the bed and ran a hand through his hair. "Fuck me." He muttered as an overwhelming sense of loneliness washed over him. Isabel was lost to him, his family had

turned their back on him and now Patience was gone. "Fuck me."
He said again as he fell back on the bed, covering his eyes with his
arm as the note floated to the floor. "What the hell do I do now?"

Isabel woke at six a.m. and showered slowly, willing the water to
wash away the fear and trepidation. No such luck. The processing center
was the place that helped you re-integrate into society. The place where
they put all the puzzle pieces together. Thoughts of this elusive man
Selene had spoken of peppered her thoughts relentlessly. *How can all of
the puzzle pieces fit into place if there were pieces missing? How does a
person become whole when there are gaps and voids?* She thought
sullenly.

She turned off the water and stepping out of the tub, toweled
herself off. Someone had brought her a change of clothes, regular clothes
and slipping into them made her feel almost human. Almost. The pants fit
well and the shirt was too big but comfy, like a much loved sweater. She
padded out into her living area and sat down to eat. Again, someone had
slipped in and left her breakfast. It annoyed her that they could come and
go as they pleased, invading her privacy.

She picked at her food and was hungry, but the roller coaster her
stomach had climbed on tossed it about making her nauseous. The food,
somewhat bland and tasteless sat in her stomach finally like a lead weight,
adding to her discomfort. At eight a.m. exactly, a soft knock sounded and
a Loram peeked in. Isabel didn't recognize the woman as being anyone
she'd seen since entering this, her private hell. "Isabel?" The woman
stepped in, tall, drop dead gorgeous and a smile that could melt an iceberg.

"Yes?" Isabel said tentatively, standing to greet the woman. "Hi Isabel," the woman said extending her hand. "I'm Patience."

11

Michael had fallen back asleep on Patience' bed, legs dangling over the edge. Morning had long since past and judging by the fading light, it was early evening. With a groan, Michael sat up, pleased to note his stomach had settled. Pins and needles started in his feet like a million fire ants winding up his calves to his knees. Gritting his teeth against the sensation, he rubbed his legs furiously until he could feel them. Standing tentatively, he stumbled towards the bathroom and stripped quickly. Showering felt good, cleared his head and made him feel a little less like the ass he'd been the night before.

Pulling on a pair of faded stone washed jeans and a black t-shirt that looked painted on, Michael examined himself in the mirror and stripped again. That was what Isabel had preferred he wore so wearing it was out of the question. Walking naked down the hallway to his bedroom he felt as if he were being watched and cursed under his breath. Closing the door behind him, he quickly pulled on a pair of camel colored khakis and a black sweater.

The lights were still dimmed throughout the house but Michael kept to the shadows none the less. He grabbed the empty bottle of Sahale brandy and placed his hand on the door knob. Just as he was about to open the door the person on the other side called out, "Michael? It's me…Darshan." The breath Michael was holding exploded from him as he tossed the bottle onto the sofa and opened the door.

"You could've called ahead Dar." Michael said as he stepped aside to let his friend in.

"Call? I've been calling since nine this morning. I wanted to see how you were doing. Yesterday must've been tough on you."

Michael took the bottle from the sofa and placed it on the coffee table. "Oh," Darshan exclaimed. "'Nuff said."

"Yeah, it was a rough one. Still is. I beat the shit out of my brother yesterday though, that felt good."

Darshan laughed and actually slapped his knee. "Wish I could've seen that." He said wistfully.

Michael shifted uncomfortably in his seat and stared down at his hands. "So what brings you to this realm Dar? He asked quietly. "Why visit me now?"

Darshan thought for a long moment and when he spoke it was with all of the authority of an Arcturian Council member. "I needed to come clean," He said and when Michael spun and raked him with a scathing glare he held up his hands defensively. "No, no, no...I did not aide and abet. Your brother acted on his own. Besides, I've been keeping something from you."

Unconvinced, Michael pushed farther back against the sofa, tense and ready to spring. "Go ahead then, come clean." He spat.

Darshan quieted his thoughts and nodded. Michael, how long have you known me?" He asked.

"Centuries." Came the curt reply.

"How well do you know me?"

"Better than yourself."

"What am I?"

Michael faltered and quickly gave the only answer he could. "An Arcturian council memb..." Michael's words dried up as Darshan shook his head slowly.

"No Michael, not a Arcturian council member. I am an Andromedan, working as an Arcturian council member. I have never been Arcturian but cannot abide to be Andromedan."

Michael stood and paced; the soft shushing of his feet on the carpet the only sound. "I'm trying to change things from the inside Michael. Trying to make what you and Isabel had..."

"HAVE!" Michael shouted and Darshan nodded.

"…Have, work." He paused then stood and smiled at his friend. "Come on Michael, let's go for a walk. I want to show you something."

Patience insisted on carrying Isabel' bag as they exited into the early morning light. Patience had stopped in and had brought Isabel a book, one she'd read a long time ago and loved. She told her she'd 'gotten lost' on her way to the admin office accidently on purpose and decided to come see her before signing in. Isabel accepted the gift and as soon as Patience had left with the promise to return, Isabel had stretched out to read. "Wait a minute," She said loudly. "How the hell did she know I loved this book?"

She turned the tome over and over in her hands. It felt good. Smelled like an old book should, dust and old paper, ink and glue. She loved the feel of a book in her hands and enjoyed reading them so much more then reading off of a micro chip stuffed into her handheld. Books were comforting and for some reason, this one felt familiar. Opening the front cover she noticed that someone had inscribed a short but poignant note on the first page. Tracing her finger across the fading words she read them aloud. "To MD. With everything I am. IS."

Isabel smiled, her initials were IS suddenly a wash of fear enveloped her and she threw down the book. IS. MD. this had to be more than a coincidence. If her initials were IS, what were the initials of this mysterious Michael? Ok, the 'M' was a no brainer but what of the D'? Panic gripped her and she grabbed the book and looked for a place to hide it. Turning in a slow circle, she spied her suitcase and moved towards it, the book like a ticking bomb in her hands.

The other Loram had given her books and told her she was welcome to keep them, maybe if she hid it in her suitcase it'd pass unnoticed. Struggling with the zipper she finally managed to open the thing and stuffed the book inside, sandwiched between her pants and toiletries. Just as she managed to close the damned thing, a knock sounded at her door, louder this time. Isabel yelped and scurried to the sofa just as Patience poked her head in. "You got everything packed sweetie?' Emphasis on the 'everything'. Isabel nodded and stood. "Cool, let's blow this pop stand then. Get you into your new digs. Looks like we're roommates for the next few weeks so let's make the most of it ok?"

Isabel nodded and sighed. This woman was peculiar to be sure; friendly but peculiar. "Ok," she sighed finally as Patience took her bags.

"You're certain you didn't forget…anything." Patience said, more statement then question.

"I'm sure I didn't forget anything." Isabel said slowly, as if talking to a mentally challenged Arcturian.

"Goood." Patience said even slower and the two women laughed. Patience moved as if she were walking on one of the three moons orbiting the planet. Slowly and deliberately, each movement exaggerated.

"Oh come on," Isabel laughed. "I've been here long enough. Get a move on woman."

Patience smiled and draped an arm across Isabel' shoulder. "Oh yeah," She sighed. "We're gonna get along just fine."

Darshan led Michael down side streets and back alley ways, Deeper and deeper into the darker, seedier parts of town. Finally, he stopped and stood in front of a dilapidated brownstone. Quietly, he stepped between the side of the house and a row of hedges. "Look." He said simply, pointing at the grimy window. "Look and see what broke me, what turned me from Fierce and proud Andromedan to full blooded Arcturian." Michael leaned into the window and drew in a shuddering breath. Never had he seen such poverty, such squalor.

Inside was a father, dressed in rags, spoon feeding his child of no more than three years. The child looked like he had a deformity, the side of his head sunken. Across the room sat a mother combing lice out of her daughter' dirty blonde hair. "By the god's Dar; who are they?" He breathed softly.

"They are," Darshan said then faltered. "They are my in-laws; my ex-wife's parents." Michael looked at his friend, expecting him to burst out laughing. Instead he nodded a sobering look on his face. "It's true," He said as he led Michael away.

"You married a Loram? Michael said once they were back on the street. "No Michael, they are Andromedan and Arcturian, one of the only mixed realm couples who've managed to have a true and lasting relationship. They were joined seven years ago and came here to hide."

"Why…" Michael said, struggling to find the words to express his horror at their living conditions.

"Why live like this?" Darshan asked and Michael nodded. "Because Michael, it's the only way they can be together; hidden, safe to live and to love. Maybe in a few years they'll be free to live a better life but for now…they have this."

They walked in silence, block after block and finally Darshan said, "That is why I am fighting from the inside, being something I am not in order to provide a brighter future for people like them; for people like yourself and Isabel." Darshan turned down a side street and stalked into a restaurant. It seemed like the weight of the world held him down, stuttered his steps. Michael followed numbly reeling from the revelation.

12

Patience held open the door for Isabel and gave her an appreciative once over as she slipped past her. They signed in at the front desk and she was given the only key card to their suite. Isabel entered tentatively, taking in everything as she moved to the center of the main living area. "Wow," She breathed. "This is impressive."

"Yeah it kinda is isn't it?" Patience noted as she dropped Isabel' bag next to the loveseat. The suite was tastefully appointed in dark mahogany and mirror. The walls a lighter shade of terracotta, the drapes a darker mix of browns and beiges.

The entire suite felt calming, just what Isabel needed. An oasis away from everything she despised. The council, her family, her thoughts. Isabel took her hand, startling her and led her through the suite. Two bedrooms, kitchen, a massive bathroom and a den. Each as exquisitely decorated as the main room. In the main bedroom Isabel noted, her personal effects had been laid out, her clothing hung in the walk-in closet. On the bed, her comforter and on that; a note.

Tentatively, she picked up the note and sat on the edge of the bed to read it. The words swam before her eyes as tears threatened to spill from her long lashes. 'Izzy, I hope this finds you well. I can't wait to see you but I can't for the first seventy-two hours. I heard what you did to mom and I can't thank you enough. Things here are kind of different but I did get that hot chocolate you raved about. You were right! This stuff has mystical properties! Hang in there sis, look at all this as a fresh start, a new beginning. I love you. Selene. She'd made it, got away. Isabel sighed and then laughed.

Patience looked at her and smiled. "You hungry?" She asked and Isabel nodded.

"Famished."

Michael pushed his plate away and stared at his friend. "How?" He asked with trepidation, not wanting but needing to hear his friends answer. "I don't know," He replied quietly. One day I'm full blooded Andromedan and the next I'm standing in the Arcturian council chamber, providing 'proof' that I was one of them. My heart, my emotions sprang to the fore, I'd never felt anything like it. One day I'm logic personified and the next my heart's overriding my common sense and everything became crystal clear."

Michael fidgeted with his napkin and sighed. "Wow." He said finally and Darshan laughed.

"Yeah...wow."

The two men left the restaurant and took the long walk back to Michael's house. The evening air held a bite but nothing more. The cloudless sky, suspended like black velvet allowed the three moons to bathe everything in a ghostly light. "You need to get back?" Michael asked and Darshan shook his head.

"Not for a few days. Thought maybe I could crash at your place."

"I'm off limits Dar, you know that. No contact is to be made by anyone on either realm. No Arcturian, No Andromedan."

"And yet here I am." Darshan said with a laugh. "Michael, seriously; do you think me dim enough to let anyone know where I was going?"

Michael allowed the silence to stretch to the breaking point before responding. "No, I don't suppose you are." He said finally.

Michael had wanted the next few days to himself, but with Darshan' sudden appearance on his doorstep, with the bizarre revelations and at his friend's insistence, Michael allowed him to stay. They watched an inane movie on television and after it was over Michael stood and without a word, stalked to his bedroom and closed the door. He stretched out on the bed and buried his face in the pillows. The tears came unbidden, and he allowed them to flow freely until sleep claimed him.

Patience sat reading as Isabel took a bath. The poor woman looked confused yet resolute, desperate yet cautious. Glancing at the clock she realized that she'd been in there more than an hour. "You ok in there?" She called and Isabel responded by opening the door to the bathroom dressed in nothing but a towel.

"I feel like a prune but yeah, I'm ok in there." She said and actually smiled. *My god, that smile.* Patience thought then before she realized what she was doing she said quietly.

"No wonder Michael loves you the way he does, that smile could melt anyone's heart."

Isabel stopped dead in her tracks, smile faltering. "What did you say?" She breathed and took a step back.

Patience stood, hands out before her like a blind woman grasping for something just beyond her reach, in this case; Isabel' trust. "Isabel, I'm sorry. I misspoke. Come here, sit down."

Isabel shook her head and pointed a finger at Patience. "Who are you? Who are you talking about? Do you know Selene? What the hell is going on?"

Patience sighed and dropped onto the sofa heavily, elbows on her knees. She pressed the palms of her hands against her closed eyelids until lights sparkled behind them and sighed. Running her hands through her tussled hair, she stared across the room until her eyes adjusted to the moonlight streaming in through the kitchen window. Turning, she gazed at

Isabel as if she was seeing her for the first time. "Ok, well the cat's out of the bag now so come here, sit, I'll do my best to explain." She said softly.

Isabel moved stiffly and sat on the loveseat opposite her and drawing her legs up under her said, "Go on, I'm listening."

Patience turned on the television and turned up the volume. She reached for a book and flipping through it, patted the seat next to her. Raising a quizzical eyebrow, Isabel unfolded out of the chair gracefully for someone dressed in a towel and sat next to Patience. "This way they'll think we're watching a movie." Patience whispered.

"They...?" Isabel said just as softly.

"There are cameras and microphones all throughout the processing center. It ensures that no one will do what I'm about to do."

"Which is?" Isabel said, staring straight ahead at the television.

"I'm going to tell you the truth about why you're here."

Suddenly Isabel didn't want to know. The abyss she'd peered into just yesterday yawned before her, calling her, and Isabel wanted to throw herself off the precipice.

Patience made a show of pointing at something in the book and laughed. It was all for show Isabel rationalized as her analytical, Andromedan mind reeled. She took the book and whispered. "What?"

"Read from here to the end of the chapter, I'll go make us a snack so everything looks normal. It'll seem like you're reading and I'm watching a movie. Go on, it's ok. I promise."

Michael awoke with the worst kink in his neck. His heart beat sluggishly and his brain refused to function. It felt as if he was shutting down physically, mentally. The only living part of him was the part he wished were dead; his tumultuous emotions. If he couldn't feel, he could live. This was a punishment far worse than death. To feel, to know, and to remember everything and to be powerless to change anything. Tentatively he pulled the picture of her he'd taken eons ago out of his dresser drawer. A glance and his heart clenched then expanded, threatening to explode. With a cry, he shoved it back into the drawer and slammed it shut.

Darshan heard Michael sobbing last night, heard him get up, and heard the cry and the slamming of the drawer. He got up from the sofa and just as he reached the door to Michael's bedroom, Michael emerged and collapsed into his friends arms. Darshan dropped to his knees under Michael's crushing weight and held his friend. "It's going to be ok," He murmured softly. "Michael it's going to be ok. We'll find a way to put everything back together, I swear it."

Michael struggled to his feet and began raging against his house. The house he'd shared with Isabel. With every beat of his heart his fists flew, smashing tables, gouging plate sized holes in the walls. Darshan watched in silence, not moving to stop him. Finally, stopping in the living room, Michael let loose a cry that drove fingers of cold fear spiking through his friend. He stood panting, surveying the carnage around him and sighed. Darshan knew then that Michael was broken. Now all that remained was to pick up the pieces and fit them back together again.

Hours later, after a meal and a shower, Michael and Darshan worked side by side silently, repairing the damage done to his house. Neither spoke because in all honesty, they would have been empty, platitudes that neither wanted to speak, neither wanted to hear. Just as Darshan was to suggest they stop and get something to drink, a soft knock sounded at the door. Michael shot Darshan a look and nodding, he slipped from the room. Michael went to the door and opened it slowly. Of all the people he thought might have come knocking on his door, she was the last.

"Hi Michael," Serenity said. "Can I come in?"

13

Isabel closed the book and rubbed her eyes. It was the book that Patience had given her, her favorite. The only difference being that in the center the pages had been removed and expertly replaced. Where one story ended, another began; a story about a man and a woman in an impossible relationship. One that was doomed to fail from the start; a story that spanned centuries. The story of an Arcturian named Michael and the Andromedan he loved named Isabel.

Patience sat stoically and stared at the television, chancing furtive glances at Isabel as she read. When she closed the book, she rubbed her eyes, stood and stretched. "I need air." She said and Patience stood.

"Go get dressed. Let's take a walk out in the garden." She said and Isabel nodded. Patience turned off the television and put the plates of food into the cooling unit. When she got to the door Isabel was there and held out her jacket for her.

"Thanks." She said and smiled a sad smile at the woman.

Isabel returned the smile and sighed. "Wow." She said softly.

"That's a sure runner up for understatement of the year." Patience laughed.

The garden was a two acre affair with every plant and tree Isabel had ever seen and then some. "Cameras...?" Isabel asked softly.

"Yes, no microphones though."

Isabel seemed to think about it for a moment then said, "The story, that wasn't...umm."

"Fiction?" Patience supplied and Isabel nodded.

"No Isabel, it wasn't. It was a history, your history with Michael."

"Why can't I remember?" She sighed and Patience took her hand.

"It's why you're here. Michael's brother who was working with your mother turned you both in. You're mind was wiped of every memory you ever had of Michael. His punishment is far worse."

Isabel stopped. "Worse? What could be worse than having someone rape your mind?"

"Michael," Patience said softly, turning to look into her eyes. "Michael was sentenced to live with his, with every memory intact, every thought, feeling and emotion; forever."

Isabel's mouth worked but no sound escaped. Her heart clenched and she moaned aloud. "No…" She said the word low and mournful. "No, no, no…oh gods that is horrific. I would sooner die than endure that."

"Michael would rather live. Live with the memory of you, with the hope that he will see you again. That everything will return to how they were."

Isabel thought of that, what a fate; and to endure it for her. "He loved me." She said softly and as gently as she could, Patience corrected her.

"*Loves* Isabel *loves.*"

"Serenity? What's wrong? Where are the kids?" Serenity smiled and chuckled.

"Yes, nothing and with a sitter." She said as she brushed past him. "I thought you might like some home cooking so I made you some. Nothing fancy, lasagna, garlic bread and dessert. A completely inadequate way of thanking you."

He took the platter of food from her and smiled as she surveyed his decimated furniture. "Hated the look or was it just not all that comfortable?" She laughed as she pointed at what remained of his sofa.

"Needed a change." He said as he placed the food on the table.

"You've made enough to feed a small army." He said and she nodded.

"You're not exactly petit." She said as she joined him.

"Dar?" He said suddenly and Serenity turned to see a tall dark skinned god approach them. Her knees went weak under his smoldering stare.

"Who have we here?" He said and Michael didn't know how to respond.

"Serenity." She said simply. "A friend of Michael's." Darshan nodded and glanced at Michael.

"Well he needs friends right now, pleasure to meet you Serenity." Her mouth went dry as if she'd swallowed a glass full of cotton so she gestured at the food.

"Sit. Food. Eat." She managed and Michael laughed. She turned and glared at him, her cheeks burning.

"Yes," Michael said to Darshan. "Sit. Food. Eat. Before she hands me my ass."

Michael watched as Darshan worked his charm on Serenity. They laughed and smiled, seemingly oblivious to his presence. Finally as he stood to clear the table, Serenity said, "I'm sorry Michael, I came here to see you and we've completely ignored you. How are you doing; other than the redecorating I mean?"

Michael shrugged and mumbled, "I'm alright." Before moving into the kitchen.

Serenity excused herself and followed after Michael, pulling him to a stop. "Michael, tell me. How *are* you?"

Michael placed the dinner plates on the counter and pulled the ambrosia she'd prepared for dessert from the fridge. "I'm dead on the inside, ruined. The black husk that used to be my heart died yesterday at noon. Is that what you want to hear?" He snarled and Serenity, at a loss for words, stepped in and hugged him.

Michael didn't feel her warmth, didn't feel the sorrow emanating from her nor the grief. He felt nothing at all and that alarmed him more than anything. He truly was dead on the inside, broken and destitute. Sighing he pushed her from him and stared at his feet. "I'm sorry Serenity, I don't know how to cope, how to move on."

"You don't." She said as she raised his chin until their eyes locked. You don't move on Michael, you stand strong, expecting the worst and hoping for the best. Everything is going to work and, *I know* you and your Isabel will be together again. That right there? That was the hope speaking. Give your hope a voice Michael, trust and believe and you'll see."

Patience led Isabel back to the suite and excused herself. Alone with her thoughts, Isabel reached for the book then thought better of it. She walked the length of the suite and back again, lost in thought. Their love was straight out of a book, something real and powerful yet she couldn't even draw on a single emotion. Not like, love or lust. Not happiness, sadness or indifference. *How is everything going to be alright?*

She thought. How can we have all of it, all over again when I feel nothing for the man? The man I can't even remember?

The whir and click of the lock drew her attention and she turned to see Patience entering the suite, arms laden with comforters, pillows and blankets.

"What's this?" She asked as Patience pushed the coffee table out of the way with her foot.

"Girl's night." She said simply. "We pig out on junk food, drink too much and I give you a mani and a pedi."

"Seriously?" Isabel said somewhat shocked.

"Seriously, now go put on some flannel pajama's and get back out here. I'll get a fire started and we'll begin."

Isabel walked from the room somewhat stunned and frowned. She didn't own flannel pajamas yet there, on the foot of her bed was the most unsightly pair she'd ever seen. Picking up the bottoms, she stared at it aghast. They were pink with big brown teddy bears playing with ABC blocks on it. *Great.* Sighing, she stripped and slipped into them. *Ok,* She admitted to herself. *They are warm and comfy. Big whoop.* But despite her recalcitrance at wearing them, Isabel felt herself smile. "Just so you know," She said as she stepped into the living room. "I look like a dork."

"Good," Patience replied. "That makes two of us."

Patience had a matching set on but instead of teddy bears, hers sported penguins in top hats sitting outside igloos. "Oh I like yours better." Patience exclaimed and clapped her hands. "Wanna switch?"

Isabel smiled and shook her head at her friends' exuberance. "No, that's ok. I'll keep mine thanks." She said as she sat on the edge of the sofa. "So what's next?" She asked and Patience frowned.

"What do you mean what's next? Haven't you done this before?" Isabel shook her head and stared at the fire. "Ok, well you're in for a treat then." Patience said, taking her hand. "Come on, down here by the fire."

Serenity doled out the ambrosia as Michael conferred with Darshan. "Sounds like your Patience didn't run out but out the door and into a world of hurt if she's caught." Darshan said as he moved back into the dining room.

"What she lacks in actual experience she certainly makes up for in exuberance." Michael said softly and Serenity perked up.

"Sounds like you're talking about my sister Patience." She said and Darshan nodded. "What?" She said as she set the bowl down on the table a little forcefully. "What aren't you saying?"

Darshan shook his head and smiled. "Nothing at all." He said and Serenity pointed the big wooden spoon at him as if it were a weapon of incredible power.

"Bullshit!" She said as her gaze swept over Michael then back to Darshan. "The look on your face said it all buster, now sit, eat and spill."

Darshan spared Michael a look and whispered loud enough for Serenity to hear. "God's man, she is exquisite. How can that look she just gave me coupled with her threat turn me on like this?"

"She's just like her sister; you wouldn't want to piss that one off either." Michael returned before he thought. Serenity' face blanched then went the brightest shade of red Michael had ever seen.

"Umm," Michael said as Serenity reached for a bowl. "Dar?" He said and Darshan, gazing at Serenity, licked his lips.

"Uh-huh?" He said as Michael backed away.

"Dar; RUN!" He shouted as he ran from the kitchen at full gallop, a bowl of ambrosia exploding against the wall where his head had been moments before.

"OW!" he heard Darshan cry from the dining room, followed by another exclamation. "Serenity please put down the bowl." Darshan said panting as he dodged spoons and bowls. Michael stood peering around the corner as Serenity unleashed furious female warfare on Darshan.

Finally, as she ran out of things to throw at Darshan, Serenity stopped, panting. "How dare you?" She said, the words clipped and tinged with frost.

"Compliment you?' Darshan offered and smiled the wickedest smile she had ever seen.

"Yeah, umm, what?" She said and Darshan laughed.

"I complimented you and you went all Holomarsten newt on me. Glad I didn't say something to anger you."

Serenity took a deep breath in then exhaled slowly. "Michael!" She shouted as she pointed at the table, a clear indication for Darshan to sit. Doing as he was wordlessly instructed, Darshan folded his hands in his lap and waited.

Michael cautiously entered the dining room and peered around the corner. "Yes…?" he said as he spied Serenity rifling through his cutlery.

"Sit." She said and Michael hurried to comply. Placing the large bowl of ambrosia between them, Serenity handed each of the men a spoon and said, "Eat."

Not needing any more encouragement than that, both men dug in. After a minutes silence Serenity said in a voice that no longer held any frost, but fear. "So, is Patience in any danger? Is she going to be ok?"

Patience finished off the avocado mask on Isabel and grinned.

"What…?" She said as she stood to look in the mirror hanging over the fireplace. "Oh gods." She exclaimed softly as she sat back down and leveled a glare at Patience who was trying her damnedest not to laugh. "I look like…" Isabel said and Patience, unable to contain herself roared with laughter.

"Fiona!" She cried as tears streamed down her cheeks. "You look like Fiona!" The puzzled look on Isabel' face sent Patience into another fit of laughter. "Old movie." She laughed. "Millennia old, Shrek, Fiona, ogres."

"Ogres?" Isabel said aghast. "I look like an ogre?" Patience barely moved out of the way as Isabel lunged for her. They struggled halfheartedly as Patience' mirth began to rub off on Isabel. Soon both women were laughing as Patience tried to explain the premise of the movie.

"I'll see if they have a copy in the archive and we'll watch it." She said finally. "You'll love it." Isabel eyed her suspiciously, doubtful that she'd enjoy a movie that was not only directed at kids but a cartoon as well.

Settling back in, Patience grabbed one of Isabel' feet and began to rub it. Instantly, all of the tension drained from her body.

"You have any more books I can read?" Isabel asked quietly as Patience' thumbs worked the arch of her foot, causing her to moan.

"I didn't bring any other." Patience said then added, "It's a better read the second time around. Most people don't get the analogy the first time out. Wait a day or two and have another go at it, I'm curious to know if you drew the same conclusions I did."

Isabel smiled, the slight upturn of her lips at the corner of her mouth brightening her features. "I doubt it, you're a Loram and I'm Andromedan; your people tend to read into things too much instead of focusing on the point."

Patience thought for a minute and pulled Isabel' other foot into her lap. "That *is* the point," She said as she worked on the ball of Isabel' foot. "I get a big kick out of hypothesizing, of pulling more out of a story than a purely clinical mind can."

"Sounds like a waste of time and energy to me. What more is needed than the absolute?"

Patience sighed and leaned back against the loveseat. "Let's see, ummm, escape?" She said as she worked on Isabel' toes, eliciting a sigh from her.

"Escape? Escape from what?" Isabel said quietly, ready to hear whatever ridiculous thing Patience had to say.

"The everyday, the ho-hum, and the monotonous grind we find ourselves in everyday. Imagine a world where absolutely anything is possible. A place with only one moon, a place where your favorite drink flows from a fountain in the middle of a park or a place where all you had to do was think of something and it appeared. Now put yourself in the middle of said world and just...imagine."

"Imagine what?" Isabel said as she tried to process everything Patience had said.

"Imagine anything silly." Patience laughed. "What would your world look like? The people, the houses, the shops."

Isabel drew in a shuddering breath and sighed. The sound was filled with all of the hope, longing and despair she felt. The moment wasn't lost on Patience; this was what she was counting on, a breakthrough

of sorts. The catalyst that would either shut down or kick start Isabel'
heart.

"Memories." She whispered as she stood and ran to her room,
slamming the door and locking herself inside.

14

Michael, Darshan and Serenity returned to the decimated
living room and sat, Serenity across from the two men. "She is not
so much in danger as she is, in a precarious position." Darshan was
saying.

"Precarious how?" Serenity asked. Her gaze bouncing
between the two. "I understand what she's doing and why," She
said as she squeezed Michaels hand. "But why would she be in
danger, or in a precarious position? What is the worst that could
happen?" She stumbled over the last question, dreading the
response. Obviously the Andromedans and the Arcturians were
very steadfast in their quest to be the one ruling realm. How far
would they go to ensure that?

"The worst case scenario would see your sister brought up
on charges by both the prefect's and the council but ultimately she
would be judged by the Loram judicial system. That being said

should either the prefect's or the council choose to, they could see her trial date drawn out for, well…ever."

Serenity reeled as if she'd been punched and stood, then sat again. She looked as if she were ready to bolt and it was Michael's hand that stayed her. She looked at him as if he'd ripped out her heart and was showing it to her. "How could you?" She whispered and Michael felt his heart break.

"Serenity…?" Darshan said quietly and she slowly turned to face him, her eyes, filled with accusation lingering on Michael. "Serenity, from what I've been told of your sister and based on *your* spirit; do you think anyone could have stopped her?"

Serenity slowly released the breath she was holding and seemed to deflate right before their eyes. Finally, after what seemed like an eternity she said, "No…no one could have. Once she's made up her mind to help someone, there is no stopping her."

Darshan smiled an understanding smile and took her hand. Serenity shuddered, his hand; warm and calloused brought her more comfort than anything she'd ever known. "We," He said indicating Michael. "Will make sure nothing happens to her. I will personally pay the center a visit tomorrow and I will check in on them; make sure that she understands that while she will only be at the center for six weeks, she needs to proceed with caution. It would be too easy to forget about the cameras and microphones, too easy to become complacent."

Serenity stared at Darshan, his words as comforting as they were bounced around inside her head, competing for space with her growing sense of dread.

"…Serenity?" Michael said. Michael was speaking to her and she'd missed it. She turned her gaze back to him and smiled a faltering smile. Her eyebrows rose, disappearing behind her bangs. "Your children? What time do you need to be home?" He asked softly.

Glancing at the digital read out on the wall she stood slowly. "Now would be good. I'm going to need a shuttle." She said as if the words were the first to issue from her mouth.

"I'll drive you." Darshan said as he stood. "Michael, get some rest. I'll see you in a few days." Then turning to Serenity he offered her his arm and smiled a beguiling smile. "Shall we?" He asked and Serenity nodded.

"Goodnight Michael," She said quietly, stooping to kiss his cheek. "Sorry about your kitchen."

Michael watched as Darshan pulled away from his house, Serenity secure in the passenger seat. Turning, he surveyed the main floor and chuckled. "I need a maid." He said to himself, his voice echoing in the open room. He shut the lights and wandered down the hall towards his bedroom, fingers trailing along the wall as he walked. He slowed as he approached his room, reached out and shut the door.

Stepping past his room, he slipped into the room Patience had occupied. It was sterile and well-kept and held no memory, no trace of Isabel. It was exactly what he needed. He crossed the room, his footfalls like thunder in the silent house and sat at the desk, intent on starting a running account of every memory he had of Isabel, and pulled a pad of stationary in front of him. Taking a pen from the drawer he began to doodle as he gathered his thoughts.

Hours passed and Michael stared down at his drawing, what had begun as an exercise in organizing his memories, in stilling his emotions and remaining in a peaceful and blank state of mind had somehow become a black and grey portrait of Isabel, her face hidden in shadow but none the less...perfect. He ground his teeth together and tore the picture from the pad. Just as he was about to ball it up and throw it out, he stopped.

Barreling from the room he hit the door to his room with the flat of his palms. The heavy mahogany door exploded inward, wooden shrapnel littering the air. The door to his closet fared no better as he ripped it from its hinges in his haste. The box was tucked in the far corner of the closet. It, contained all of the pencils and water colors he'd put away eons ago. Behind the box were the canvases and easels he'd abandoned.

This box held promise and purpose. It held peace of mind and the only thing that would soothe the beast that raged within. Hefting the box, he moved to the living room and placed it on the loveseat. Returning to the room he pulled three easels out of the closet and set them up one in each corner, each facing the other.

Hanging the canvases he set out pencils on one, water colors on the other and finally his acrylics on the third.

Moving like a man possessed, Michael moved from one canvas to the other and deftly began the process of bringing three completely different works of art to life, three portraits of his Isabel. One of her lounging naked, the way he remembered her the day it ended. One, a simple reproduction of her face and the last, of them together, back to the artist as they walked hand in hand away from everything and everyone.

15

Patience tidied up the suite before locking herself in her own room. While the evening hadn't gone as she'd expected, it hadn't been a disaster either. She worried that she'd pushed Isabel too far but she needed a reaction out of her and sometimes, full tilt boogie was the way to go. Still she worried. Worried that left alone with her thoughts, Isabel might shut down. Mind made up, she left her room and knocked on Isabel' door.

"Come in." Isabel said her voice barely above a whisper.

Patience slipped into the room which was bathed in the unearthly glow of the planets three moons. Isabel lay on her side, back to the door clutching a pillow. "My room's cold." She said as she moved silently next to the bed. "Mind if I..."

Isabel remained silent for a moment. Just long enough to acknowledge the fact that Patience' room was fine and she was just worried about her. Without turning, she reached behind her and pulled the comforter aside, a silent invitation.

Patience slid beneath the comforter and hesitated before closing the space between her and Isabel. The moment she did, the moment her arm wrapped itself around Isabel' waist, Isabel dissolved into silent tears. Patience held her as her body shook with every gut wrenching sob. "Why...? How...? I don't understand." She whispered too low for the microphones to pick up.

"It's ok baby," Patience soothed quietly. "It's ok. Everything's going to be ok."

Patience held Isabel as she cried herself to sleep and only then did she allow herself the luxury of sleeping herself. Once sleep claimed her, Patience dreamt of joy and happiness, pain and despair. No one in particular held fast to those emotions, they seemed to soar on gossamer wings and float on the darkest waters. Melding together in bright and vivid colors only to bleed into a wash of grays and blacks.

Morning came slowly like a lover on tip toe. Kissing them softly with bright sunlight and warm breezes. Patience stretched and sat up slowly, Isabel at her side nestled in a cocoon of comforter and sheets. She peered at the digital read out on the wall and sighed. Seven fifty and it was already seventy four degrees outside. The day was gearing up to be another scorcher. "Isabel...?" She said as she shook her arm. "Isabel, we have to get up. Counseling starts at nine and I want breakfast."

"Have some for me," Isabel murmured from beneath the blankets. "'Nother half hour."

Patience thought for a moment and shrugged. She'd order breakfast and shower quickly before it got here. That'd allow Isabel her extra half hour and they'd still have time to make it to counseling. Slipping from the bed, she strolled out to the living area dressed in her flannel pajamas. Rounding the corner, she'd almost missed the man standing before the picture window staring out at the garden. "I was wondering how long you'd sleep." The man said as he saw her reflection as she'd passed by. Turning he was all smiles and extending his hand he said, "My name is Darshan and I have a message from your sister."

Patience stared at the man but remained where she was. Eyeing him suspiciously she said, "What's her name?"

"Serenity." Darshan replied calmly. "Although with her fiery temper I'd be more inclined to call her The Agitator." The last was said with a smirk.

"What does she look like?" Patience demanded.

"Before or after she assaulted me with a perfectly good bowl of ambrosia and kitchen implements?" Darshan said dryly.

Patience stepped towards him, menace thickening the air between them then faltered. "Ambrosia...? Serenity made ambrosia?" Darshan nodded and gestured at the sofa, a clear invitation for her to be seated. Patience shook her head and turned away, disappearing around the corner. Seconds later she breezed past him as she slipped a jacket on and stepped out into the garden.

Darshan smiled and turned to follow her. *Smart cookie this one,* He thought to himself as he quickened his pace to catch up to her. Once they were past the main area of the garden she turned to face him, their noses mere inches apart. "Explain." She said vehemently. Darshan held up his hands palms out and took a step back.

"Easy there tall, blonde and good looking. I'm one of the good guys. Serenity showed up at a mutual acquaintances house to see how he was doing, I was there." Patience became very still, heart clenching at the thought of Michael in that house, alone. Of course Serenity would visit. They had someone in common they cared about…her.

She sat on one of the benches that lined the trail and made room for Darshan. He sat quietly and smiled at her. "She's well, so is Michael…sort of. He had a break down yesterday but after the meal your sister brought us, he seemed to calm a bit. I just came here to thank you and to remind you to always be on your guard."

"Thank me for what?" Patience said as she stared out into the tree line. "On my guard against what?"

Darshan straightened in his seat and draped an arm along the back of the bench running his fingers up and down her arm. Giving anyone watching the illusion of two lovers having a chat. Patience felt heat radiating off of him, sending goose bumps crawling down her flesh. "For what you're doing for our friends and to be on your guard because the Loram that run this center have eyes and ears everywhere, constantly changing their monitoring patterns. One slip and it's all over."

Patience leaned into the man and rested her head on his shoulder, her arm on his thigh. "You're welcome and I will." She said quietly. They sat silently, each lost in thought. Finally, Darshan moved his arm and slowly stood.

"Your sister…" He began and Patience stared up at him expectantly. "Your sister is…I was wondering…It's just that…" He pinched the bridge of his nose and squeezed his eyes shut in a physical display of the frustration he was feeling. Patience smirked and recovered a millisecond before he fixed his gaze on her.

"You're laughing at me." He said without a hint of arrogance. Patience shook her head, eyes wide and hid her smile behind her hand. "Oh gods!" Darshan said as he stared up at the canopy of trees above them. "Your sister," He said and Patience giggled. "I like your sister. It's maddening but true. One glance and my brain ceased to function. One word and I became undone."

"Yes." Patience said as she stood and strolled past Darshan.

"Yes…? Yes what?" He called after her before following.

"Yes you can date my sister silly." She said casually then laughed.

Michael sat on the floor, a bottle of D'Icily wine between his legs, the canvases surrounding him. He didn't look at them, didn't want to see them. The ice he felt forming in his heart had begun to melt as he wove his magic with brush and crayon but now that he was finished, he felt ice water coursing through his veins. Tipping the bottle to his lips he drank, the cool liquid soothing his parched throat, setting fire to his belly. Standing with a grunt, he took the first of the canvases and pinned it to the wall. The second and third followed suit and he quickly prepared three more.

He worked and drank. Fire and ice coursing through his veins. Heart filled with hope and hopelessness. Finally, too drunk to see straight he staggered into the kitchen and picked up the phone. Vision blurred he had to dial the number three times before getting it right.

"Can I help you?" The gravelly voice on the other end said, clearly not pleased with being woken up.

"Opie?" Michael slurred. "Opie that you?"

There was silence on the line and finally, with a sigh, "Hang on I'm switching phones."

Michael waited. The sounds of covers rustling and a murmured *'its ok go back to sleep'* the only sounds. Finally as Michaels eyelids began to close "Yeah Michael, it's me. By the gods man you're risking my family by calling here."

"I want it to end Opie; I want it over with. No more, no more, no more." Michael said quietly. "You know someone, you always know someone."

Opie sat quietly and listened to Michael's breathing. "How many you had Michael? How wasted are you?" He asked.

"Not enough…never enough."

"I might know someone, go to sleep Michael, wake up tomorrow and really think about what you're asking. I'll find a way to contact you tomorrow. Until then, never call me here. I have a wife and children to worry about."

Michael hung up and leaned his head against the wall, legs rubbery, back stiff, head pounding. With a grunt he pushed away from the wall and stumbled forward until he reached the spare room. The room was pitch dark, almost as dark as Michael's soul but not quite. Thoughts of Isabel tormented him as he tossed and turned then, just as the first rays of the morning sun began to seep through the curtains, Michael let sleep claim him.

16

Isabel sat quietly, hands folded in her lap as the counselor read through the report on her desk. Finally, after what seemed like an eternity, she closed the file and smiled at her. "So," She began, her voice roughened by years of smoking. "Looks like everything went well."

Isabel furrowed her brow and sneered at the woman. "Went well? Having your mind raped and being left with massive gaps equals well?" The woman stood and moved to the seat next to Isabel. She went to take her hand but stopped short when Isabel snarled, "Do. Not. Touch. Me." The woman sat back and stared at Isabel as if she suddenly didn't know how to proceed.

"Acts of aggression, even verbal aggression is frowned upon." She said finally.

"And touching someone without their express permission is sexual harassment." Isabel shot back. "Try to touch me again and I'll have you before the council."

The woman reached across the desk and pulled the file into her lap. Flipping it open she scanned the first page and frowned. Isabel was indeed a council member and a powerful one at that. "Fine." She said as she returned behind the desk. "My apologies council woman."

Isabel shifted in her seat, assuming a more relaxed pose. "So why am I here exactly? I doubt that you're going to fill in the blanks so what is the purpose of this?"

"The purpose of counseling is to ensure that you are able to reintegrate into society seamlessly. To return to your life healthy and whole."

Isabel barked laughter and shook her head. "Whole? *Whole*?" She said and laughed again. "Like a pie with a bunch of finger holes punched into it?"

The counselor shook her head and made a note in Isabel' file. "I'm getting the feeling we booked this session prematurely so I propose we cut it short. Go and enjoy the rest of your day, shop, nap or read. We'll reschedule for a week tomorrow."

"Oh," Isabel said with a smile. "Have I been dismissed?"

The counselor glared at Isabel for a moment before saying softly, "Yes you've been dismissed.

Michael woke up feeling like he'd been eaten by a bear and shit down the wrong side of a mountain. His brain rattled around inside his head, a sure sign of dehydration. He struggled out from under the blankets and shuffle stepped out to the kitchen. Taking a lukewarm bottle of water from the counter he stepped out into his back yard and sat wearily on the steps. The sun forced his eyes closed but warmed him almost instantly. There was something to be said about Scandia, it was warm all of the time.

Polishing off the bottle of water, Michael squinted at his neighbor, an older gentleman who'd lost his wife decades ago. The man raised his hand in greeting and Michael waved him over. He disappeared behind the bushes and reappeared moments later, his t-shirt plastered to his chest and back. "Good morning Michael." He said. "You look like hell."

Michael smiled and moved so he could sit next to him. "Thank you for noticing." Michael said. "You're still fat."

The older gentleman laughed and jabbed Michael in the ribs. "I know," He wheezed. "But I can fix fat, you can't fix ugly."

Michael smiled and sighed. "Penny for your thoughts?" His neighbor said and Michael frowned.

"What's a penny?"

"What's on your mind Michael, tell me what has you binge drinking, destroying your home and crying in the middle of the night."

Michael winced and instead of answering, asked a question of his own. "How did you cope with loosing Bindy, Graham?"

The old man sighed and leaned against the railing, staring out at nothing as if drawing on fading memories. "I didn't." He said finally. "I wake up missing her and go to sleep loving her more and more. Is something wrong with you and your Isabel?"

Michael almost retreated back into the house, back into himself and whatever bottle he could find but Graham's hand stayed him. "They found us," He said finally. "My own brother turned us in, Isabel' memories of me have been erased. I'm left with them...all of them...for always"

Graham whistled long and low. His heart ached for Michael, for Isabel. "I'm so sorry son," He said quietly. "Losing Bindy was hard... *is* hard but she's gone...forever. There is no bringing her back. I can't imagine what you're going through."

The two sat in silence, neither sure of what to say. Then, as if hit by divine revelation, Graham stood and marched down the steps. Turning to face Michael he put a hand on his shoulder and said, "Stay strong Michael and for the love of all things good don't do anything foolish. I'll be back in a few hours."

Michael peered at the man and nodded. "Ok Graham," He said without conviction. "I'll see you then."

Patience was just wandering through the suite, naked from her bath and heading for her room when Isabel entered. "Wow…" She said startled and Patience turned, face turning beet red.

"Oh shit, sorry." She laughed as she grabbed two throw pillows from the sofa and covered herself, barely.

"Didn't know this was a clothing optional suite." Isabel laughed and sank into the plush loveseat.

"Aren't you supposed to be in counseling?" Patience asked as she backed away towards her room.

"Time off for good behavior." Isabel said as Patience disappeared into her room.

"Bull shit." Patience said as she stepped back out into the hallway dressed in a terry cloth robe.

"Yeah," Isabel said. "Bull shit."

"Oh god what did you do?" She said as she plopped down next to her.

"Nothing, I didn't like the woman, don't like to be touched and when she realized that I was a member of the council she suggested that I spend the rest of the day shopping."

"Isabel…" Patience groaned. "You didn't."

"Piss off the woman? Yeah I kind of did. Explain something to me Patience, how does one become whole again when they're missing decades of their lives? What's the plan? Feed me bullshit and lies so I fill in the gaps with someone else's memories?"

Patience scrubbed a hand across her face and glared at Isabel. "I'm going to get dressed. We'll go out and get a bite to eat, shop." Without waiting for a response, she stood and marched back to her bedroom.

Isabel sat and waited in silence. She'd upset the only friend she had and that bothered her more than the counselor she'd met with. She listened as Patience bustled around her room and relaxed a little when she emerged with a grin plastered on her face. "Patience I'm…" She began but Patience cut her off with a wave of her hand.

"Come on, let's get shopping woman." She said and Isabel clammed up. Standing, she followed her out of the suite and hurried to catch up. "Food first?" Patience asked and Isabel nodded.

"Yeah, being a bitch makes me hungry."

Michael kept himself busy by scraping ambrosia out of the carpets and off of the walls. He stayed in the kitchen, unwilling to enter the living room. Finally after what seemed like hours, he inspected his handy work and allowed himself a slight smile. The kitchen was gleaming, every surface scrubbed, everything in its place. He caught himself as he reached for a half bottle of Merlot and took a bottle of water from the fridge instead. Sitting at the table, he eyed the living room, littered with paints, crayons, pencils and canvases.

With all of the resolve of a dead man walking, he entered the room and began taking down the portraits. Moving slowly, he handled them reverently, rolling them and placing them in tubes. He gathered his supplies and placed them in the box. The easels he'd used went back into the closet. Michael vacuumed and polished what was left of his furniture and even drew open the curtains, opened the windows. The main floor looked less like a battle field and more like his home by the time he was done.

The sun had peaked and crested, sending golden rays through the windows in the living room. Michael sat wearily on the sofa, and stared out at the Loram who were going about their day. Mothers with their kids, businessmen, seniors…all oblivious to the immortal who lived next door. The immortal that'd been weighed, measured and found to be lacking. The immortal whose punishment was unjustified and wrong. Why the members of either council couldn't see that was anyone's guess.

He understood that both realms had reason to fear. Neither were great in number and to loose a member to mortality and eventually death meant a shift in power. The Arcturians reviled the Andromedans and vice versa but what he couldn't understand was why, if two people loved each other, they weren't allowed to express their love as they saw fit. If it meant leaving their realms and becoming joined, it was their right. The councils, ruled over by families had determined that the other was beneath them and so, they enforced the rules with swift and determined cruelty.

Pushing himself off of the sofa, he'd made it halfway to the bathroom, ready for a shower when a soft knock sounded at his door. He turned and was half way there when the door squeaked open and Graham stepped inside. "Care to keep an old man company?" He asked and Michael nodded.

"Sure, need to shower first. Have a seat Graham, I'll be right out." The old man nodded and sat in the kitchen, uncertain as to whether or not this, his plan would work. Twenty minutes later, Michael emerged, showered and dressed. "So...?" he asked as he walked towards the man. "What were you thinking?"

"Well, your place looks like hell and since I need to pick up a few things, I thought you might like to join me."

Michael smiled and said, "Sure, shopping sounds like fun."

Patience cleared the way for Isabel as if she were visiting royalty. They'd stopped for lunch and were floating from store to store, a member of the center's team pushing a cart with their purchases following behind. Before stepping into a lingerie shop, Patience turned and held up her hands. "That's far enough buddy." She said to the young man. "You can take those back to the center, we'll pick them up at the front desk." The youth nodded and turned the cart, ambling away, relieved that patience had cut him loose.

Turning, Patience smiled a wicked smile at Isabel and slipped her arm around her shoulders. "Ready for some fun?" She asked and Isabel rolled her eyes.

"By fun you mean…?" She said and peered at Patience.

"Time to try on some knickers. I'm curious to see what floats your boat."

Isabel worried her lower lip with her teeth and finally a grin appeared, lighting her eyes with mischief. "Alright Captain Underpants," She said with a laugh. "Come on, show me those granny panties."

"Ouch!" Patience laughed as they stepped inside the store. "That hurt, I'll have you know I'm more of an Underoos kinda gal."

The Loram running the store were put through their paces as Patience and Isabel tried on everything ranging from the boring to the scandalous. Finally after a two hour long marathon of shopping, Patience produced her card and paid for their purchases, a bra and two matching panties. It turned out Isabel did have a wicked side, a side that included foregoing undergarments of any kind.

They left the store arm in arm, laughing at the destruction their whirlwind shopping spree had wrought. Patience was trying to steer Isabel back towards a shoe store they had missed while Isabel, intent on a black cherry, white chocolate latte pulled her along. Turning a corner they never saw the men before they ran straight into them. Isabel hit the one in front of her with such force that she stumbled backwards. His hand shot out and he righted her before she fell. "Sorry," She said breathlessly as she looked up at him. "That was clumsy of me."

Michael stared at Isabel and felt the world tilt sideways.

"Oh gods!" Graham swore at the same time Patience said a little less delicately,

"Oh fuck."

Isabel stared at the trio and frowned. The tall good looking one looked like someone she should remember but couldn't place. The older one she recognized instantly and stepped in to hug him. "Graham, oh my god it's been ages." She cried as she pulled him into her arms.

"How's that good looking neighbor of yours? Oh what was his name again? Marc? Marlin? Matthew? Oh crap I can't remember."

Michael felt the blood drain from his face, felt his heart constrict and swayed on his feet. Graham steadied him casually and smiled at Isabel. "I'm sorry sweetheart, I'm in a bit of a rush. Come see me sometime?"

"Of course," Isabel said softly. "Your friend looks like he needs to sit or eat or something so we won't keep you. It was nice umm, bumping into you." She said to Michael with a twinkle in her eye. "Maybe I'll see you again sometime."

Michael swallowed and nodded. "Sure…" He managed before Patience linked arms with Isabel and whisked her away. "That sounds wonderful." He finished quietly.

Graham steered Michael away, leading him back to the food vendors. He deposited him into a chair and patted him on the back, a distinctly fatherly gesture. "Stay here Michael, I'll be right back." Michael nodded and propped his head up on his hands, his heart pounding relentlessly against his rib cage, his mind spiraling downward despite the hope and joy he felt at having seen her. "Here," Graham said, pushing a tray of food onto the table. "Eat this." Michael, never lifting his head began to eat the food placed before him. His movements mechanical and automatic.

"I'm sorry Michael," Graham said around a mouthful of food. "I never realized, never thought…"

Michael shook his head and looked up at the old man. "It's not…it's ok…you didn't know." He said as tears began to spill from his lashes. "Gods Graham; I can't do this. I can't keep on going. You lost Bindy but she's not coming back. These…these encounters can happen at any time. It feels like everything good inside of me has died. My heart, my soul. How do I kill the memories?"

Graham stared at Michael, chewing over his thoughts much in the same way he did his lunch. He swallowed and took a sip from his cup and sighed. "You don't kill them Michael, you hold onto them. I lost Bindy, yes, and it kills me a little more every day. Isabel is still out there, obviously. If she were dead so would be hope, but she isn't. Hope springs eternal, latch onto it. Believe Michael. Believe that in the end everything is going to work out as it was meant to be. The Andromedans and the Arcturians be damned, umm no offense."

Michael pushed his plate away and drained his cup slowly. "None taken." He said wistfully. "Truth be told I would have preferred to be raised Loram."

Despite her best efforts, Isabel was incapable of steering Patience back towards the food vendors, back towards Graham and his mystery friend. In fact, Patience had declared their day shopping over and almost forcibly dragged Isabel along with her back to their suite. Finally and with every ounce of the Andromedan council member within her Isabel planted her feet, an immovable object. Arms folded across her chest she refused to budge. "Why?" She asked for the hundredth time. "Why can I not go back and see Graham? He is a friend."

Patience stared down at Isabel, a determined set to her lips, eyes blazing with anger, or was it fear? Finally, she reached out and took Isabel' arm. "Come with me." She said quietly. "So we can speak without being overheard." Isabel nodded tersely and followed her as she wound her way through the throng of shoppers. Finally, Patience pulled her into a bath house just outside the shopping center. She paid for the use of a private sauna and pulled Isabel along behind her.

The women stripped down, stored their clothing in a locker and pushing her in front of her, Patience directed Isabel towards the hot tub. Inside she prayed that the gurgling of the water and the hiss and knock of the steam in the pipes would drown out their conversation. Once settled in, Patience turned to Isabel and stared at her.

"Well...?" Isabel said and Patience said softly.

"Keep your voice down. What I am about to tell you, you must accept as the truth. Do not react in any way, remain stoic. Do you understand me?"

Isabel nodded, swallowing past the lump in her throat and said "Yes, I understand."

Patience settled in behind Isabel and began rubbing her shoulders, intent on whispering in her ear as she did. "You recognized Graham." She said and Isabel nodded.

"Yes, he's an old friend."

"And the man with him?" Patience asked, her heart pounding in her chest.

"No, never seen him before." Isabel said then added with a smirk. "He's cute though."

Patience drew in a shuddering breath and in a voice barely above a whisper said, "Isabel...that was your Michael."

Graham and Michael took the shuttle back home and parted ways, Graham with Michael' solemn vow to keep the faith and to not do anything stupid. Michael wandered through his house fighting the urge to race back to the shopping center and claim Isabel for his own again. Common sense, a long lost companion reared its head and bellowed. She didn't know him, recognize him. Taking her would be more kidnapping than rescue. He had to trust Patience and Darshan. Trust them to do whatever it was they were doing. Trust that he would one day be with Isabel as they were meant to.

Oscar Percival Edwards or Opie for short, approached Michael' house cautiously. During their trial, Isabel' and Michael' closest friends were forbidden to have contact with them for six years thereby condemning them to a solitude so complete as to be cruel. The Andromedan and Arcturian councils had agreed on that one point above all others. Being caught here would sentence Opie to a long prison term, but Michael was his friend. A friend who'd done more for him than any other so here he was, about to knock on his door.

Michael stood and opened the door, fully expecting to see Darshan or Serenity or even Graham. When he saw Opie, he blanched. The previous night' discussion rushing to the forefront of his thoughts. "I'm kind of a target standing out here Michael. Mind if I come in?" He said when Michael hesitated. Michael stepped aside and let the man in, shutting the door closed behind him. "I can't stay but I've done what you've asked…here." He said as he handed Michael a vial of clear blue liquid. Michael took it numbly and stared at the liquid. "If you drink it all Michael, every last drop, oblivion is yours for the taking." Opie said and turned to go.

"I saw her today Opie," Michael said softly and Opie froze in his tracks. "At a shopping center. I was out with Graham and she was there, shopping with a…friend."

Opie turned and faced his friend, a pained expression on his face. "And…?" He said and Michael seemed to fold in on himself.

"And it was as if I were a ghost. She didn't recognize me at all."

Opie ran a hand through his hair and blew out the breath he'd been holding. He didn't know if he should say he was sorry or relieved and after a moment's hesitation, decided on the gentler of the two. "I'm sorry Michael." He said and once the words left him he knew beyond a shadow of a doubt that he was. "I'm sorry for you and Isabel both. If two people had been meant…"

Michael cut him off with a snarl and clenched his fist about the vial. "We *are* meant to be together Opie." He said and felt his heart constrict, expand. "We are." Opie nodded and inclined his head.

"Are," He whispered. "I wish you well Michael. I won't be able to see you again. I hope you understand."

Michael nodded and watched as his friend took his leave.

Isabel tensed as Patience' words sank in. Michael, the Michael from the story; *their story* and she hadn't recognized him at all. Oh, he was beautiful to look at. A fantastic specimen of male flesh, but without her memories of him…

Patience cleared her throat and sighed, her breath feathering Isabel' back and shoulders. "What are you thinking?" She whispered and Isabel sagged against her.

"I don't know." She admitted. I don't know what to think."

Patience moved out from behind Isabel and took up a position directly in front of her. Isabel looked as if someone had punched her in the gut. Pain and frustration marked her face, radiated from her in wave after wave. "Give it time Isabel," She whispered. "We will get through this I promise."

"And what?" Isabel said softly. "My memories are gone. What kind of future do we have if he remembers everything and me nothing? What are we supposed to do? Sneak around and make new memories and pray we aren't caught again?"

"There are worse things than starting over Isabel, far worse things."

"Like…?" Isabel said as she sank deeper into the water, her nose and eyes the only thing above.

"Like never loving, being alone…forever, unwanted and unloved."

Isabel' eyes widened and she sat up a little straighter. "Oh gods Patience, I'm so sorry, I didn't know." She said as realization sank in. Patience was one of those, the unwanted and unloved.

Patience waved a hand in the air dismissively and smiled. "You don't get to turn this around on me Isabel. This is about you, not me." She said with a hint of anger and bitterness. "My life or lack thereof is no one's concern but my own. " Then a thought occurred to her, she mulled it over for a moment then took Isabel' hand.

"Tell me about the procedure. Tell me everything. What was it like?" Isabel, without hesitation said, "I was standing on the precipice of an abyss, thoughts and memories slipping away, tumbling over the edge. I wanted to follow them, to get them back but I couldn't bring myself to jump…I wasn't sure what would happen if I did."

Patience stood abruptly, the water sluicing off of her lithe body and extending a hand, motioned for Isabel to follow. "I have an idea, it'll need some planning but I think it might work. You game?"

Nodding, Isabel put on her 'brave' face and took the Loram' hand. "Sure," She said. "I want to remember, no matter the cost."

Michael sat and fidgeted with the vial, holding it up to the light, studying it. His heart was torn. Hope and despair, constantly at war. With a sigh, he shoved it into the pocket of his jacket and took his keys. It was a short drive to Fulcrum Point and he thought that to thank Serenity properly, he'd pick up some flowers and maybe some more toys for her children. He stopped at the mall he and Patience had visited and hurried to find a florist. That done, he went back to the store where they had bought the kids their toys and grabbed the first age appropriate toys he could find.

As he approached the house he'd purchased for them, he noticed a car in her driveway, Darshan' car. He smiled and shook his head. He'd known there had been chemistry between them but couldn't imagine a lasting relationship. Dar was Arcturian through and through. Immortal. Serenity was Loram and since birth had a death sentence hanging over her head. Accident, disease, age…eventually one or the other would catch up with her and that would be the end. *Let them be happy for the time they're allotted.* He thought and taking his gifts, approached the front door.

"Michael!" A voice said from behind him. A voice he knew well, one he loathed. Turning Michael faced his brother and a contingent of Arcturian security officers.

"Bryce." Michael said with venom shooting through his veins.

"Arrest him." Bryce said and several of the officers moved forward. Suddenly the front door opened and Michael was pulled inside. Slamming the door Darshan said, "Take him downstairs. Take the children with you." Serenity nodded, her lips a thin line as fear washed over her. Taking a deep breath, Darshan opened the door and faced Bryce and his men.

"Dar...?" Bryce said and he cut him off.

"That would be councilman Darshan to you." He said and stood in the doorway, filling it with his mass.

"We're here for Michael." Bryce said as he gestured at the men around him.

"On what charges?" Darshan spat, the words a foul thing on his tongue.

"This house was purchased by Michael for the sister of the woman tending to Isabel at the center. That is far too coincidental if you ask me."

"Prove it." Darshan said and Bryce laughed.

"I don't need to, I purchased it for him."

Smoothly, as if Bryce had just told him the time, Darshan leaned against the doorframe and smiled. "Well, we're just about to sit down for dinner so you might want to come back another time."

"That is not going to happen." Bryce said and looking at his men said, "Take the house, arrest everyone inside...including Councilman Darshan."

Darshan slipped inside and bolted the door. He was halfway across the room when it exploded inward. He turned and snarled at the men who hesitated briefly before charging him. Minutes later Darshan, Serenity, Michael and the children were handcuffed and led from the house. Michael apologized over and over again as they were placed in separate Security Council vehicles. He'd blown it. Destroyed any chance of seeing Isabel again, destroyed friends and family in the process. In that moment, he knew what he had to do. It was time to end it once and for all.

Patience left Isabel in the suite and encouraged her to take a nap. She promised that she would return as soon as she could, assuring her silently that she would set her plan in motion, a plan Isabel knew nothing about.

Isabel slipped into bed and tried to nap but couldn't. Her thoughts were on that delectable man, her man. He had looked so broken, panicked and she understood why. He remembered her, their time together. Remembered the quiet times, the intimate times. What torture that had to be. She moved to the living area and turned on the television. Settling down, her head on a pillow she was just dozing off when something on the screen had her pushing into a seated position, hand reaching for the remote.

There on the screen was Michael, being led away in handcuffs with a family following behind. Reaching for the remote she turned up the volume as dread washed over her. "…breaking the conditions of his sentence, Council member Michael Cross is being remanded into custody to await the council' final verdict. There is a good chance he will be sentenced to the same memory erasing procedure his outlaw Andromedan partner, Council member Isabel Snow was. Stay tuned to this channel for further updates."

Isabel stood, then sat again; then standing, ran to the bathroom. She vomited, dry heaving until she thought her heart would burst from the effort. Clutching the edge of the sink, she pulled herself to her feet and ran the water, cupping her hands beneath the frigid stream. Splashing water on her face, she scrubbed a towel across it, smearing her make up. She was just about to run from the center when the door opened and Patience stepped in.

"What's wrong?" She said when she saw Isabel. "What happened?"

Isabel ran into her arms and began to sob. "They've taken Michael," She choked out. "They're going to erase his memories."

Michael sat in an interrogation room and waited. He'd been there for hours and the bastards had taken his coat and along with it, the vial in the pocket. Finally, Bryce entered followed by an armed guard. "You are such an idiot." He said as he took a seat across from Michael who remained silent. "Purchasing a home for the sister of your accomplice. It was only a matter of time Michael, before we found something to crucify you with."

Before he could respond the door opened and an older gentleman entered. Councilman Trey, the head of the Arcturian council. "Out." He said to Bryce with a look of disgust. "You too." He added, nodding at the guard.

Michael watched as Bryce gathered his things and exited the room, his tail between his legs. He almost smirked but couldn't bring himself to do it. Councilman Trey sat in the place Bryce had vacated and leaned his elbows on the table. He looked at Michael and sighed. Michael, wilting under his gaze, stared at the tabletop.

"I've turned off the recording devices and the cameras so we can speak freely." He said and Michael lifted his eyes to the councilman.

"Why?' He asked and Trey smirked.

"Because Michael, believe it or not, there are some of us out there who want to see you happy. Who believe there is more to life then what we believe in and hold fast to."

Michael sat back in the hard wooden chair and truly looked at the man. "It's over." He said finally. "She doesn't remember me, recognize me and I'm to be sentenced to the same fate which, truth be told would be easier then living with my memories."

"It's not over Michael," Trey said. "In fact it's only begun. I had a visitor today, a mutual acquaintance if you will." Michael raised an eyebrow, a silent entreaty to continue.

"Patience came to see me. She seems to think that we can restore Isabel' memories and I tend to agree."

"How do you know Patience?" He asked and Trey smiled.

"She did me a favor once, I'm simply returning it."

Michael stood and paced for a minute before asking, "How?"

Trey looked at Michael, determination in his eyes, in the set of his jaw. "Patience believes that as a persons memories are sailing over into the abyss, if that person were to follow, to take a leap of faith if you will, the memories can be restored. I believe that if you and Isabel were to undergo the same procedure, together, your combined memories would bond you, restoring you both."

Michael let the words sink in and thought furiously. "What are the risks?" He asked. "If there is any risk to Isabel I won't do it."

"Patience is talking to her as we speak. If she agrees to this Michael..."

"The risks Trey, what are they?"

"Oblivion for you both." Trey admitted softly. "This in my opinion, is preferable to the alternative." The ensuing silence thickened the air, making it hard for Michael to breathe.

Finally, like a man defeated Michael said, "What do I do?"

"Go through it again?" Isabel said as she walked alongside Patience in the garden.

"Yes but, together. Melding memories, joining you both in spirit." Patience said softly. "If it doesn't work though, it means the end. You need to know that Isabel. There are risks."

Isabel laughed and Patience looked at her as if she'd lost her mind. "Greater risks then covertly keeping a relationship going with two realms gunning for you? Greater risks then living a life that is a lie, broken and missing portions of it? I'm ok with the risks Patience. Oblivion is a better option then what I've been left with."

Patience nodded. Here was a woman who couldn't remember the man she loved but was resolute in her decision to be restored to him. That, in her estimation should be the definition of love. "Ok," She said finally. "Ok, we move ahead as planned. During your next counseling session I want you to hit that bitch with every memory of Michael that you can. Make some up if you have to. We need you to convince her that you remember."

Isabel turned and faced her friend. "This is stressful, so stressful. I need to blow off some steam. Want to have some fun with this?" She asked and Patience pursed her lips.

Tapping her chin with her finger she smiled slowly and said, "I've always been a shit disturber, what did you have in mind?"

"I'm going to go lay down for a few hours…"

"Oh that sounds like fun." Patience deadpanned and Isabel laughed.

"You go find something to do, when you come back I'll 'wake up' and will have had a dream, one in which I remembered *everything*."

Patience snickered and said, "Let the games begin then. I hope you're a good actress."

"I guess we'll find out." Isabel said as she walked back to the suite, Patience in tow. Once inside she said with a stretch and a convincing yawn, "I'm going to take a nap."

"Uh, ok…I'll go and check out the library here. I need a few good books to keep me company if you're going to nap your life away."

"See you later?" Isabel said and Patience laughed.

"Duh, we're roomies." Isabel waited for Patience to leave and for the second time in as many hours, slipped beneath the comforter.

Darshan, Serenity and her children were released at Trey' order and Michael escorted back to his cell. The Councilman had arranged for him to have his memories erased in three days, plenty of time for Patience and Isabel to do what they needed to do. Upon hearing that she 'remembered', she'd be sentenced to have her memory wiped again. Trey would then suggest that they be wiped together, a fitting punishment for the 'criminals' they were. If all went well, they would be restored and not destroyed.

If all went well.

Michael lay on his cot in the cell, his dinner left half eaten on the floor beside him. His heart swelled with hope, only to have despair sink its razor sharp talons in, cutting. There were far too many 'what ifs', too many variables. Too much that could go wrong.

He thought of the vial that Opie had brought him, what happened to it? Had they found it? Did they know what it was? The hours crawled by slowly, dragging out his torment, his anguish. Finally, he drew on every precious memory of Isabel he had. He focused on them as Trey had instructed him to. Having them fresh in his mind would facilitate the transfer.

From their first meeting to their unexpected encounter earlier today and everything in between, Michael painted the memories with vibrant colors. Every emotion linked to those memories lanced him. Pain, joy, despair, happiness…on and on it went but he embraced them, clutching them like a drowning man did the life preserver thrown to him. Finally, Michael slipped into a dreamless sleep. The first in ages.

Patience entered the suite three hours later, just as they'd planned. Isabel sat on the sofa, legs under her, clutching a pillow and rocking herself. Tears had ruined her make up, her eyes red and swollen. "Isabel…? What's wrong, what happened?"

Isabel turned her face to Patience, lips quivering, then in a movement so quick Patience had trouble following it, she threw herself into her arms. "Oh gods Patience, I remember, I remember everything. I remember Michael!" She cried and Patience held her as her words were reduced to sobs.

Patience staggered under her weight, her heart breaking with every cry, every sob. She half carried her to the sofa and sat holding her.

Moments later the door opened and her counselor walked in with a medical team in tow.

"We'll take her." She said crisply and Patience knew exactly why Isabel despised her. The medics took Isabel from Patience' arms and strapped her to a gurney. "Thank you for your help Loram Patience, obviously the procedure didn't take so we will have to do it over. Your presence is no longer required."

Patience nodded and went to pack her things as they wheeled Isabel out of the suite. Heart pounding, she packed quickly and remembered to take the book she had given Isabel. 'No evidence' Trey had told her and Patience wracked her brain for anything else that might be construed as 'evidence'. Finally, she surveyed the room and picking up her bags, exited the suite. At the beginning she believed that she would be able to get Isabel to remember, now everything was out of her hands and depended on nothing more than luck and timing. With a sense of foreboding, she stepped onto a shuttle and headed back home.

Michael went through the motions of existing within his cramped ten by ten cell. Thanks to his brother, he wasn't allowed visitors or anything of comfort. Without books or a television he was left alone with his thoughts, thoughts that ran the gamut from the fantastic to the desperate. Three times a day he was brought food by a silent Loram who'd been instructed not to speak to him. Three times a day the Loram returned to collect his tray. He had counted the holes in the ceiling tiles twice and had numbered the bricks. *How the hell do people cope with life sentences?* He thought bitterly. Then again, they had books and luxuries Michael would never be afforded.

Isabel was interrogated regarding her memories and drawing from the place where she'd committed 'their story' to memory, she told them everything. The counselor frowned with every tale, the look on her face souring, angry. Never before had anyone been able to remember and the fact that this one had, galled her. "I'm scheduling you for another treatment." She said and Isabel smirked.

"You make it sound like I'm going to get my hair colored."

The woman scowled at her and tsked. "Don't get smart with me Council woman. Your status means little if anything at all to me. Councilman Trey' orders are all I care about."

Isabel stood and glared down at the woman. "If you think the Andromedan council is going to sit back and let you or the Arcturians do anything to me, you are sadly mistaken." She said through gritted teeth.

The woman smiled a terrifying smile at her and pulled a paper from her folder. "Your beloved council has already signed off on it," She said sweetly. "See…? That's your mother' signature right there, next to councilman Trey's" Isabel froze then smiled.

"Fine, but remember this; my vengeance will be swift and ugly and you've made it to the top of my list."

"I'm not going to worry about it," The woman said as she motioned the medics forward. "You will have no memory of this meeting…none at all."

The day Michael was to be brought in for the wipe started like any other. He was to be brought to the center at three p.m., then exiled to the remotest of places on the planet. At eleven-thirty his cell door opened and in stepped Bryce. "What do you want?" Michael said, rising to his feet.

"Last supper." Bryce said with a smile holding out a tray of food. "After today you won't be remembering me."

Taking the tray, Michael sat and leveled his brother with a glare. "Thank the gods for small mercies." He said quietly.

Isabel had showered and changed and was waiting for the transport that would take her back to the facility. Her nerves were getting the better of her and she twisted a napkin in her hands, slowly shredding it. The door to her room opened and her sister Selene walked in and unceremoniously dropped onto the seat next to her. "I'm glad to see you Izzy." Selene said as she laid her head on her shoulder. "I'm told they're wiping all of your memories, not just the ones of Michael." Isabel sat quietly and took her sister' hand. "I'm going to miss you." Selene said as tears burned in her eyes.

Bryce watched as Michael ate in silence, never acknowledging his brother' presence. Finally Michael stood and tossed the tray in Bryce' lap. "Take it and go." He said and with a smirk, Bryce stood and stepped to the door. The guard on the other side opened it for him and closed it as soon as he was on the other side. Bryce turned and stared at his brother' back.

"That vial we found in your pocket, what was that Michael?" He asked and Michael turned. "I don't know what you're talking about." He said and Bryce smiled.

"Oh. well we'll find out what it was soon enough," He said. "Wonder what it does."

"None of my concern." Michael spat and Bryce laughed.

"Oh Michael, it *is* your concern. You see, I added it to your water." He said as he tipped Michael' empty glass.

Isabel was wheeled into the center of a large sterile room and left alone as the technicians moved about setting up. There was a bed next to hers, empty, awaiting the arrival of the man she loved. She glanced around and noticed a curtained off area. When she'd spied it, as if on cue, the curtain parted revealing three rows of seats. A viewing area where Andromedan', Arcturian' and Loram' were to gather to witness the enacting of her and Michael' punishment. One by one the seats filled, her mother and father, her sister, Michael' brother and friend Darshan. It seemed like everyone was present, eager to watch the show.

Trey opened the door to Michael' cell to find him face down on the floor, his skin a sickly blue. "Get a medic!" He shouted at the guard outside as he turned Michael over. Michael' heart beat a thready rhythm in his chest. With every passing second it grew weaker and weaker. "Michael...why?" Trey asked and Michael shook his head, the motion causing him to groan loudly.

"Bryce..." He said weakly. "Poison..." He finished. The effort of expelling those two words costing him. Trey pulled him into his lap and held him as Michael breathed his last. An immortal gone, killed by his own brother.

Isabel watched as Darshan conferred with another of the Arcturian' and slammed his fist into the wall just to the right of the man' head. He stormed out of the room and appeared in the chamber moments later. The guards stopped him before he reached Isabel and pulled him away screaming. "Do it Isabel...jump!" He cried as they dragged him away. Isabel looked about, confusion and terror riding her hard.

"It appears that Michael was found dead in his cell this afternoon." A voice said through the speakers. Then after a pause, "Begin the procedure." Isabel immediately caught a whiff of the scent of 'sleep' as the Loram called it and in seconds, she was standing on the precipice, her memories tumbling over the edge. Without a second thought she stepped off the edge, into oblivion. Once and for all, reunited in death with her Michael.

"A glooming peace this morning with it brings; the sun for sorrow will not show its head. Go hence, to have more talk of these sad things: some shall be pardoned, and some punished: for never was a story of more woe than this of Michael and his Isabel."

.

Manufactured by Amazon.ca
Bolton, ON

16984979R00074